## "Do you want me to kiss

His voice was husky to his own ears.

"Yes." Then she seemed to realize what she'd revealed.

Their kiss was better than he remembered, even better than his imagination. Her lips were tender and hot. She tasted sweet. And when he probed with his tongue, she answered in kind, tipping her head and leaning against him.

Her body was soft and warm, her curves smooth against his angles. He wrapped his arms around her, enveloping her while the kiss went on. Arousal throbbed deep and hard within him, and his mind galloped ahead to an image of a large bed, with her naked body wrapped around his.

Why couldn't it always be like this? Why did they have to fight? She was smart and sassy, and probably the most interesting woman he'd ever met. She was certainly the most exciting.

And then reality slammed into him.

They did have to fight. And no amount of wishing would change that.

His interests were diametrically opposed to hers. He absolutely couldn't sleep with her—not with the secret he was keeping right now.

\* \* \*

*From Temptation to Twins* is part of the Whiskey Bay Brides series:

Three sisters find love on the shores of Whiskey Bay.

Dear Reader,

Welcome to the first book in the Whiskey Bay Brides series! Growing up, I spent a lot of time in the Pacific Northwest. I've always loved the soaring cliffs, the salt tang of the ocean and the roar of spectacular storms that crash against the rocky shores. So, Whiskey Bay seemed like a perfect place to set a tempestuous wedding series.

In *From Temptation to Twins*, newly credentialed chef Jules Parker returns to Washington State against her family's wishes to revive her grandfather's quirky seafood restaurant. There she runs afoul of her family's archenemy, millionaire restaurateur Caleb Watford. His planned five-star restaurant will annihilate her dream, while her little eatery has the power to stop his project in its tracks.

If Jules leaves, then Caleb wins. But he also loses everything. Because his enemy has become the love of his life, and she's carrying his twins.

*Barbara*

# BARBARA DUNLOP

---

# FROM TEMPTATION TO TWINS

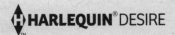

HARLEQUIN® DESIRE

Recycling programs
for this product may
not exist in your area.

ISBN-13: 978-0-373-83864-6

From Temptation to Twins

Copyright © 2017 by Barbara Dunlop

Printed in U.S.A.

www.Harlequin.com

*New York Times* and *USA TODAY* bestselling author **Barbara Dunlop** has written more than forty novels for Harlequin, including the acclaimed Chicago Sons series for Harlequin Desire. Her sexy, lighthearted stories regularly hit bestseller lists. Barbara is a three-time finalist for the Romance Writers of America's RITA® Award.

## Books by Barbara Dunlop

### Harlequin Desire

*One Baby, Two Secrets*

### Colorado Cattle Barons

*A Cowboy Comes Home*
*A Cowboy in Manhattan*
*An Intimate Bargain*
*Millionaire in a Stetson*
*A Cowboy's Temptation*
*The Last Cowboy Standing*

### Chicago Sons

*Sex, Lies and the CEO*
*Seduced by the CEO*
*A Bargain with the Boss*
*His Stolen Bride*

### Whiskey Bay Brides

*From Temptation to Twins*

Visit her Author Profile page at Harlequin.com, or barbaradunlop.com, for more titles.

For Mom

# One

*Here Comes Trouble*

The man all but filled the open doorway of the dilapidated Whiskey Bay Crab Shack. His feet were planted apart, his broad shoulders squared and his no-nonsense chin was tipped up in a challenge.

"Is this supposed to be a joke?" he asked, his deep voice booming through the old brick building.

Jules Parker recognized him right away. She'd expected their paths would cross, but she hadn't expected open hostility—interesting. She hopped down from where she was kneeling on the dusty old bar and stripped off her leather work gloves.

"I don't know, Caleb," she answered as she sauntered toward him, tucking the gloves into the back pocket of her faded jeans. "Is there something funny about dismantling shelves?"

He squinted at her. "You're Juliet Parker?"

"You don't recognize me?"

He held out a level hand, moving it up and down, judging the distance to the ground. "Last time I saw you, you were—"

"Fifteen years old."

"Shorter. And you had freckles."

She couldn't help but smile at that. "Okay."

That was nine years ago. Did he think she wouldn't have changed?

His gray eyes hardened. "What are you doing?"

She pointed over her shoulder with her thumb. "Like I said, dismantling the bar shelves."

"I mean, what are you doing *here*?"

"In Whiskey Bay?" She and her younger sister, Melissa, had arrived yesterday, having planned their return for over a year.

"In the Crab Shack."

"I own the Crab Shack." At least, she owned half of the Crab Shack. Melissa was her partner.

He pulled a piece of paper from his back pocket, brandishing it in his fist. "You *extended* the business license."

"Uh-huh." The fact clearly upset him, though she wasn't sure why.

"And you *extended* the noncompete clause."

"Uh-huh," she said again. The noncompete was part of the original license. Everything had been extended.

He took a step forward, all but looming over her, and she was reminded of why she'd had a schoolgirl crush on him. He was all male then, and he was all male now—hot, sexy and incredibly good-looking.

"What is it you want?" he asked in that low, gravelly voice.

She didn't understand the question, but she wasn't about to back down. She squared her shoulders. "How do you mean?"

"Are you playing stupid?"

"I'm not playing at anything. What's *your* game, Caleb? Because I've got work to do here."

He glared at her for a couple of beats. "Do you want money? Is that it? Are you looking for a payout?"

She took a stab at answering. "The Crab Shack's not for sale. We're reopening."

The Whiskey Bay Crab Shack was her grandfather's legacy. It was hers and Melissa's dream, and also her deathbed promise to the grandpa she adored. Her father hated the idea of the family returning to Whiskey Bay, but Jules wasn't thinking about that today.

Caleb's gaze covered the room, seeming to dismiss it. "We both know that's not happening."

"We do?"

"You're starting to annoy me, Juliet."

"It's Jules. And you're starting to annoy me, too." His voice rose in obvious frustration. "Are you telling me it's not about *this*?"

She looked to where he was pointing out the window.

"What?" she asked, confused.

"This." He headed out the door.

Curious, she followed and saw the Whiskey Bay Marina. It looked much as it always had, although the caliber of vessel berthed there had gone up. The pier was lined with sleek, modern yachts. Beyond the marina, in what had always been raw land, there were two semitrailers with a front-end loader and a bulldozer, plus a couple of pickup trucks.

Whatever was being built there likely wouldn't be as attractive as the natural shoreline, but it was far enough away that it shouldn't bother their patrons after they re-opened. To the south of the Crab Shack, it was all natural vistas. The signature, soaring cliffs of Whiskey Bay were covered in west coast cedars and wax-leafed salal shrubs. Nobody could build on the south side. It was all cliffs and boulders.

Jules made a mental note to focus the views on the south side.

"I don't think that's going to bother us too much," she said.

Caleb's stunned expression was interrupted by Melissa's arrival in their mini pickup truck.

"Hello," Melissa sang out as she exited from the driver's side, a couple of hardware store bags in her arms and a bright smile on her face.

"Do you remember Caleb Watford?" Jules asked.

"Not really." Melissa set the bags down on the deck and held out her hand. "I remember the Parkers hate the Watfords."

Jules knew she shouldn't smile at her sister's blunt statement. But the revelation couldn't come as any surprise to Caleb. The feud between their grandfathers and fathers was well-known. It was the likely reason Caleb was being so obnoxious. He didn't want the Parkers back in Whiskey Bay. Well, that was too bad.

Caleb accepted Melissa's hand. "Either you two are the best actors in the world…"

Melissa gave Jules a confused glance.

"Don't look at me," Jules said. "I haven't the slightest idea what he's talking about. But he's ticked off about something."

"You see that?" Caleb pointed again.

Melissa shaded her eyes. "Looks like a bulldozer."

"It's my bulldozer."

"Congratulations…?" Melissa offered hesitantly, her confusion obvious.

"Do you two have any idea what I do?" he asked.

"No," Jules answered.

She knew the Watfords were rich. They owned one of three mansions set along the cliffs of Whiskey Bay. Besides the mansion, the only other house on the bay was the Parkers'. It was just a regular little old house. Her grandfather had lived there for nearly seventy years before he'd passed away.

"Do you drive a bulldozer?" Melissa asked.

"Seriously?" Jules asked her sister, finding it impossible to imagine Caleb as a heavy equipment operator. "The Watfords are mega wealthy."

"He could still drive a bulldozer," Melissa said. "Maybe he likes driving a bulldozer."

"Rich guys don't drive bulldozers."

Jules pictured Caleb behind a big desk in an opulent office. No, that wasn't quite right. Presiding over a construction site, maybe? He could be an architect.

"Have you ever seen *Construction Vacation*?" Melissa asked.

"The TV show?"

"Yeah. All kinds of guys, rich, poor, whatever. They come on the show and play with heavy equipment. They like it. It's a thing."

"Well, maybe on a lark—"

"Stop!" Caleb all but shouted.

Melissa drew back, clearly shocked.

"He's been like this ever since he showed up," Jules said.

"Like a bear with a hangnail," Melissa muttered.

"I don't think that's a metaphor," Jules said. "Bears have claws."

Caleb was glancing back and forth between them. His skin tone seemed to have gone a little darker. Jules decided it might be good to let him speak.

"I own and manage the Neo chain of seafood restaurants. That—" he stabbed his finger in the direction of the bulldozer "—will be the newest location."

Both women looked along the shore, and Jules realized why Caleb was so annoyed.

"Oh," Melissa said, pausing for a short beat. "Except you can't build it now because of the noncompete clause in our business license."

"It was *supposed* to expire on Wednesday," he said.

"I saw that when we renewed."

"Now I get it," Jules said to him. "I can see why you'd be disappointed."

"Disappointed?" Caleb caught the beer Matt Emerson tossed him from the wet bar at opposite side of the marina's sundeck. "I'm a million dollars into the project, and she thinks I'm *disappointed*?"

"You're not?" TJ Bauer asked evenly as he popped the top of his own beer.

The three men were on the deck that sat atop the Whiskey Bay Marina office building. A quarter moon rose in the starlit sky, while the lights of the pier reflected off the foamy water eddying between the white yachts.

Caleb shot TJ a glower.

"Do you think this is about your dad?" Matt asked.

"Or your grandfather," TJ added, bracing his butt against the rail. "This could be your chickens coming home to roost."

"They're not my chickens," Caleb said.

"Does *she* know that?" Matt asked.

Caleb couldn't believe Jules was capable of executing such a nefarious revenge plan.

"Are you suggesting she figured out that I was planning to build a Neo location at Whiskey Bay, waited until the last possible moment, the fortieth anniversary of their grandfather's business license, to extend the noncompete clause and shut down my project so I'd lose a fortune, in retaliation for the actions of my father and grandfather?"

"It would earn her a significant score on the evil-genius meter," TJ said.

"Your ancestors were pretty evil to her ancestors," Matt said.

Caleb didn't disagree with that. His grandfather had stolen away the woman Felix Parker loved, while his father had ruined Roland Parker's best chance at a college education.

There wasn't a lot about either man that made Caleb proud. "I didn't do a thing to the Parkers."

"Did you mention that to Jules?" Matt asked.

"She's sticking to her story—that she had no idea I wanted to build a restaurant of my own."

"Maybe she didn't," TJ said. "You know, this wouldn't be the worst time in the world to take on investors."

"This would absolutely be the worst time in the world to take on investors." Caleb had heard the pitch from TJ before.

"One phone call to my clients, Caleb. And seventeen Neo locations across the US could become forty Neo locations around the world. A million-dollar loss here would be insignificant."

"Read my lips," Caleb said. "I'm not interested."

TJ shrugged. "Can't blame a guy for trying."

"Then call her bluff," Matt said, crossing the deck

and dropping into one of the padded chairs surrounding a gas fire pit.

"She's not bluffing," Caleb pointed out. "She already extended the noncompete clause."

"I mean pretend you believe her. That she's only after her own business interests, and this isn't some warped revenge against your family. See if she'll be reasonable about coexisting."

TJ moved to another of the chairs. "I see where he's going. Explain to her how Neo and the Crab Shack can both succeed. If she's not out to harm you, then she should be willing to discuss it."

"They serve different market niches." Caleb sat down, thinking there might be merit to the strategy. "And where they overlap, one could be a draw for the other."

"Cross-promotion," TJ said.

"I'd be willing to push some customers her way."

"Maybe don't make yourself sound so arrogant," Matt said. "I don't think women like that."

"Aren't you supposed to be the big expert on women?" TJ asked Caleb.

"Jules isn't a woman," Caleb said. But even as he spoke, he envisioned her sparkling blue eyes, her billowy wheat-blond hair and her full red lips. Jules was all woman, and that just made things more complicated.

"I mean," he continued. "She's not a woman in the way you're thinking about women. Not that she's not good-looking, she is. Anybody would tell you that. But that's irrelevant. It's irrelevant to the situation. I'm not trying to date her. I'm trying to do business with her."

"Uh-oh," Matt said to TJ.

"That's trouble," TJ said to Matt.

"It's not like that," Caleb said. "The last time I saw her she was fifteen."

TJ grinned. "And that was a logical comeback to *what*?"

"She was a kid. She was my neighbor. And now she's a thorn in my side. This has nothing to do with, you know, our recent discussions about the two of you getting back into the dating pool. How's that going, by the way?"

Both men grinned at him. "You think we're going to let you change the subject that easily?"

"Either of you dating?" Caleb asked. "Are you? Because I had a date last weekend."

Matt had just made it through a bitter divorce, and TJ had just passed the two-year anniversary of his wife's death. Both had committed to living Caleb's bachelor lifestyle for the next year. And Caleb had committed to helping them achieve it.

"Hey, Matt?" came a female voice from below on the pier.

"Speaking of women…" TJ said, interest perking up in his voice.

"Speaking of *not* women." Matt muttered under his breath as he rose to his feet.

"Who is she?" TJ asked, standing to look over the rail.

"My mechanic." Matt raised his voice. "Hi, Tasha. What's going on?"

"I don't like the sound of MK's backup engine. Can I have a day to tear it down?"

Through the rails, Caleb could see a slender woman in a T-shirt and cargo pants. She wore a pair of leather work boots. And she had a ponytail sticking out of the back of her tattered baseball cap.

"It's booked out starting Sunday."

"That gives me all day tomorrow," Tasha called back. "Perfect. I'll make sure she's ready."

"Thanks, Tasha."

"*That's* your mechanic?" TJ asked as he watched the young woman walk away.

"You want to date my mechanic?" Matt asked.

"She's pretty cute."

Matt laughed. "She's tough as nails. I wouldn't recommend her as a starting point."

"You calling dibs?"

"Fill your boots, brother. She'll eat you for lunch."

Caleb couldn't help but grin. "Should we go into the city and hit a club tomorrow night?"

Whiskey Bay was less than two hours from the nightlife of Olympia and it sounded like TJ and Matt could use a little push into the social scene. Caleb would be more than happy to forget his own problems for an evening.

"I'm in," said Matt.

"Sounds great," said TJ.

Caleb finished his beer. "In that case, I'm going home to strategize." He rose. "I like your idea to test Jules's sincerity. I'll do it in the morning."

"Good luck," Matt called.

Caleb took the stairs to the pier then left the lights of the marina behind him on the walk home.

Whiskey Bay was characterized by stunning steep cliffs. There was very little land at sea level, just an acre or so under the marina and another parcel of a similar size where Caleb intended to build Neo. The Crab Shack was located on a rocky spit of land to the south of the marina. It had been closed now for more than ten years, since Felix Parker had grown too old to run it.

Four houses sat on the steep rise of the cliff. Matt's was directly above the marina. TJ's was a few hundred yards to the south, then came the Parkers' small house, with Caleb's house last.

Back in the '50s, his grandfather had built a small place similar to the Parkers'. But while the Parker place had remained intact, the Watfords had rebuilt numerous times. After his grandfather's death Caleb had bought the house from the rest of the family, gradually renovating it to make it his own.

There was a path halfway up the cliff that connected the four houses. Caleb, Matt and TJ had installed solar lights a few years back, so walking after dark was easy. Caleb had passed below the Parker house thousands of times. But in the five years since Felix Parker had moved to a care home, there'd never been a light on there.

Tonight, it was lit. Caleb could see it in the distance, filtered by the spreading branches of cedar trees. As he grew closer, the deck came into view, and he had a sudden memory of a teenage Jules. It had to have been her last summer visiting her grandfather. She'd been dancing on the deck. Dressed in cutoff shorts and a striped tank top, her hair up in a messy knot, she was dancing like nobody was watching.

He could see her freckles. That's how he'd remembered she'd had freckles. The sunlight had glowed against her blond hair and her creamy skin. She'd been far too beautiful, and far too young. He'd felt guilty for even looking at her back then. He'd been twenty-one, building his first Neo restaurant in San Francisco.

"Spying on us?" Jules suddenly appeared on the trail in front of him.

"On my way home," he answered, quickly pulling himself back to the present.

She wasn't wearing cutoffs, and no tight striped tank top either. Thank goodness. Although her blue jeans and cropped white T-shirt weren't exactly saving his sanity. In fact, it was worse, because she was all grown up now.

"You're standing still," she pointed out.

He went with a partial truth. "I'm not used to seeing lights on in your house."

She glanced up at the deck. "I guess it's been a while."

"Quite a few years." He gazed at her profile. She was quite astonishingly gorgeous. He couldn't remember ever meeting a woman so beautiful.

"Did you know your family sent flowers?" she asked. "When my grandfather died."

"I did." It had been Caleb who'd arranged it.

"Sent my dad off the deep end, I tell you."

Caleb felt a twinge of regret. "I hadn't thought of that."

She turned to look at him again. "So it was you?"

"Was that a test?"

"I was curious. It didn't make sense that your dad would have sent them."

"No, it wouldn't." Caleb's father had once been arrested because of an altercation with Jules's father, Roland. Caleb had never heard all the details, but his father had often railed about the overreaction of the authorities, and how it was Felix Parker's fault they were called in the first place.

"He might have sent a brass band," Jules mused.

"I don't know what to say to that." Caleb wondered if she was looking for an apology.

"It was a joke."

"Okay. It seemed a little…"

"Inappropriate? To acknowledge your father might have wished my grandfather dead?" She shrugged her slim shoulders. "We can pretend if you want."

"I meant to joke about your grandfather's death at all."

"He was ninety. He wouldn't mind. In fact, I think he'd like it. You're still mad at me, aren't you?" She tipped her head to one side.

Heck, yes, he was still mad at her. But he was also massively attracted to her. Gazing at her in the dim glow of the trail light, anger was a pretty difficult emotion to dredge up.

"We can pretend I'm not," he said.

She smiled, and his chest contracted. "You *do* have a sense of humor."

He didn't smile back. He hadn't been joking. He was perfectly prepared to pretend he wasn't angry with her.

She stepped unexpectedly closer. "I used to have such a crush on you."

He stopped breathing.

"I have no idea why," she continued. "I barely knew you. Only from afar. But you were older, and it was summer, and I was nearly sixteen. And I'm sure it didn't hurt that our families were feuding. Nothing like the Montagues and the Capulets, or the Jets and the Sharks, to get a young girl's heart going. It's kind of funny now that you—" She blinked at him. "Caleb?"

He couldn't kiss her. He couldn't. He could not…

"Caleb?"

There was no way she was doing this by accident. She had to guess what it would do to him, to any mortal man. She truly was an evil genius.

"You know exactly what you're doing, don't you?" he managed to force out, annoyance in his tone.

She searched his expression. "What am I doing?"

The woman deserved an acting award.

"Putting me off balance," he said. "Dancing around on your balcony, tight shorts, tight shirt—"

"What? Dancing where?"

"You're twenty-four years old."

"I know that."

"You're standing out here in the woods, alone, telling a grown man that you once had a crush on him."

Her expression fell, and she took a step back. "I thought it was a sweet story."

His voice came out strangled. *"Sweet?"*

"Okay, and a little embarrassing. I wanted to open up. I was trying to get you to like me."

He closed his eyes for a long moment. He couldn't let himself believe that. He couldn't let her get under his skin. He didn't know what to do with this, what to do with her, how to put her in any kind of context. "I'm not going to like you."

"But—"

"You should go."

"Go?" She actually sounded hurt.

"I think we're on two completely different wavelengths."

She didn't answer. The woods around him fell silent.

He opened his eyes to find her gone. He breathed a sigh of relief. Then the relief turned into regret as he second-guessed himself. He could usually read the signs with women—tell the difference between flirting and an innocent conversation. With Jules, he couldn't.

"You told him you'd had a crush on him?" Melissa asked from the bottom of the stepladder the next day.

Jules removed the next in a cluster of '50s movie star

portraits that hung on a wall of the restaurant. "I was trying to… I don't know." She'd had more than a few hours to regret her words.

"Did you not think it would sound flirty?"

Jules handed the portrait of Grace Kelly down to Melissa and reached for Elizabeth Taylor. "I didn't mean for it to be flirty."

"It was flirty."

"I realize that *now*."

"What were you thinking *then*?"

"That it would be charming. I was being open and honest, sharing a slightly embarrassing story. I thought it might make me seem human."

"He knows you're human."

"In the end it was just humiliating." Jules handed down the Elizabeth Taylor.

"So, you learned something." Melissa crossed the room to set the portraits in a cardboard box on the bar.

"I learned that he has zero interest in flirting with me."

"I was thinking maybe a broader point about relationships, time and place, and appropriate comments."

Jules climbed down and moved the ladder, settling it into place where she could read the next three portraits. "Oh, that. No."

Melissa grinned. "Tell me more about the crush. I wish you'd told me about it back then."

"You were too young."

"It still would have been exciting."

It had certainly been exciting for Jules. "I was fifteen. He was tall, and he shaved, and he lived in a mansion on the hill. And I was fresh out of grade nine English class. Between the Brontë sisters and Shakespeare, I spun a pretty interesting fantasy."

"I don't even remember him from back then."

"That's because you were only twelve."

"What I remember most is Grandma's hot chocolate. It was so nice, coming here, spending time with her, especially after Mom died."

"I miss them both."

Melissa gave Jules's arm a squeeze. "Me, too. But I don't miss the squirrels waking us up in the morning."

Jules handed Audrey Hepburn to Melissa. "I hated those squirrels."

"You really should have thought of that before we moved back here. They're going to wake us up every morning."

"Do you think we could livetrap them, relocate them like they do with bears?"

"I don't see why not."

Jules thought about it for a moment as she handed down Jayne Mansfield. "I wonder what we'd need for bait."

"Going fishing?" The sound of Caleb's voice startled her, and she swayed, grabbing the top of the ladder to steady herself.

"Whoa." Caleb surged toward her.

"Steady girl," Melissa said.

"I'm fine." Jules regained her balance.

She focused on his forehead instead of meeting his eyes. She'd pretend nothing awkward had happened last night. Hopefully, he'd play along and they could both ignore it.

"Should you be up on that ladder?" he asked.

"I was fine until you scared me." Jules turned back to her work and reached for Doris Day.

"You were talking about fishing?"

"We were?" Jules couldn't figure out why he thought that.

"You said we needed bait," Melissa put in.

"Matt can take you fishing," Caleb said. He was hovering beside Melissa, looking like he wanted to take over the operation. "Do you need a hand with that?"

"Why are you suddenly being nice?" Jules asked as she handed over the next portrait.

She'd prefer it if they were cordial to each other. But after their argument yesterday and their encounter last night, she'd expected him to avoid her, not to drop by and pretend they were friends.

"I'm not being nice," he said.

"Who's Matt?" Melissa asked as she crossed the room with Doris in her hands.

"He owns the marina." Caleb took over from Melissa and braced both sides of the ladder.

"All those yachts?" Melissa asked.

"He has a charter service."

"Out of our price range," Jules put in. She could only imagine the exorbitant cost of renting one of the lavish-looking yachts.

"He won't charge you."

Jules took a step lower on the ladder, expecting Caleb to move back and give her room. "We're not going fishing."

"Let's not be hasty," Melissa said.

"I can set it up." Caleb didn't move.

Jules turned before she took another step down. Deciding she'd prefer to face him while edging into his space.

"We're far too busy to fish," she said, meeting him at eye level.

"Exactly how long would we need for a trip like that?" Melissa asked.

"How are you not suspicious of this?" Jules spoke to

Melissa but kept her gaze locked on Caleb. "An enemy bearing gifts?"

"I'm not your enemy." Caleb's deep voice seemed to rumble through her. There was a challenge in his gray eyes. One more step down, and she'd practically be in his arms.

She wasn't going to be the one to back down. She took the final step. "So why are you here?"

"I wanted to talk to you."

"About what?" She told herself to ignore the sizzle of arousal that skipped across her skin. He was a great-looking guy, and she had some emotional baggage where it came to him. But she could handle it. She could easily handle it.

He drew a deep breath, his broad chest expanding. A few more inches and they would be touching. She wondered how he'd handle that. She should make it happen and find out.

"The contractor's here," Melissa said, as a vehicle engine sounded outside in the parking lot.

"You need me?" Jules made to move, thinking she'd probably just been saved from...something with Caleb.

"Nope. I'll just show him around," Melissa said and headed for the door.

"We don't need to be competitors." Caleb firmed his stance as he spoke to Jules.

"We're not competitors." She wondered how long he intended to keep her trapped. She eased slightly forward to test his boundaries. "I have a noncompete agreement, so you can't build Neo."

Caleb leaned in himself, as if he could read her thoughts. "Neo's not your competition."

"I know it's not. Because it doesn't exist."

"I mean, if it did exist. We'd cater to a different clientele."

"The Crab Shack caters to seafood eaters. What does Neo do?"

"Neo's high-end. The Crab Shack is casual."

"What makes you say that?"

He seemed surprised by her words. He glanced around the building, taking in the aging brick, the torn linoleum and the rustic wood beams. "It's humble, basic, kitschy. Don't get me wrong—"

"How could I take that wrong?" She crossed her arms, and her elbows touched his chest. She tipped her head, recapturing his gaze and letting her annoyance tighten her expression.

"If you *were* to go high-end," he said.

She waited. She couldn't believe he hadn't backed off yet.

Instead, he increased the connection between them, his chest pressing along the length of her forearms. It was a firm chest, a sexy chest and an amazing chest. For a second, she lost her train of thought.

"If you were to go high-end," he said. "We'd be complementary. We could feed customers to each other. You've seen it, a restaurant district or an auto mall. We could become a seafood restaurant cluster—*the* place to go in greater Olympia for terrific seafood."

"That's pretty good."

"So you're interested?"

"No."

"Why not?"

"It's a pretty good argument, Caleb. It's not true, but A for ingenuity."

Something flashed in his eyes. It was either admiration or annoyance, maybe a bit of both. "There are examples of it all over the world."

"Neo's a nationally known and renowned chain. You'd annihilate the Crab Shack."

Melissa's and the contractor's voices were muffled as they talked outside on the deck.

"You're not going to agree to this, are you?" Caleb asked.

"No."

"We're not going to be friendly?"

"I'm afraid not."

"Okay." He nodded. He let go of the ladder and rocked back, breaking their contact. "I guess I'll go back to my corner and come out swinging."

She wasn't disappointed, she told herself. And she definitely didn't miss his touch.

"But first," he said, surprising her by reaching back to cup her cheek with his palm. "Since I probably can't make the situation much worse…"

His intent was clear. She told herself to say no, to turn her head, to step sideways. There was nothing stopping her. She was free to move and shut this down.

But she didn't. Instead, she surrendered to nine years of fantasy and parted her lips as he closed the space between them.

# Two

Before his lips even touched Jules's, Caleb knew he was making a huge mistake. He also knew he didn't care.

He'd lain awake half the night thinking about her, picturing her on the trail outside her house, reliving her saying she'd had a crush on him. He should have kissed her right then. Any other man would have kissed her right then.

Now her cheek was soft against his palm, warm and smooth. He edged his fingers into her silky hair, and his lips finally covered hers. He kept the kiss soft. He wanted to devour her, but he didn't want to scare her, and he sure didn't want her to push him away.

Her lips softened. They parted. He firmed his grip, anchoring her mouth to his, while his free hand went around her waist. Desire pulsed through his body, arousal awakening his senses. He gave in to temptation and touched his tongue to hers.

She moaned, and his arm wound around her, bringing their bodies flush together. He deepened the kiss, bending her slightly backward. His body temperature rose, and he could feel the pulse of the ocean, or maybe it was the beat of his heart.

Melissa's voice penetrated from outside, saying something about the roof. Her footsteps sounded on the deck. A man's voice rose in response to her question.

Jules's hands went to Caleb's shoulders, and she gave the slightest push.

He reacted immediately, pulling back, her flushed cheeks coming into focus, along with her swollen lips and glazed blue eyes.

He wanted it again. He wanted more. He absolutely did not want to stop.

"I've made it worse," he said, half to himself.

"We can't do that," she said, obviously voicing her own train of thought.

"No kidding."

"I can't trust you."

"You could have said no." This wasn't all on him.

Her smile looked self-conscious. "I know. I'm talking about more than just the kiss."

"Tell me why?" He didn't know why he cared, but he did.

"Why I can't trust you?"

"Yes."

She thought about it for a moment. "I can't trust you, because I can't trust you."

He wasn't buying it. "That's a circular argument. You're too smart for that."

"Okay," she said, drawing back against the ladder. "I can't trust you because you're a Watford."

He knew he should walk away, but his feet stayed stubbornly still. "You barely know me."

"I know your family."

"That's not the same thing."

"I know you want me to compromise my interests."

"Not really," he said.

She cocked her head and sent him a frown of disbelief.

"Only a little bit," he amended. "But it'll work in the long run. I know it'll work in the long run. For both of us."

"Are you lying to yourself or just to me?"

"I'm not lying."

"You definitely inherited it," she said, apparently growing tired of waiting for him to back off. She slipped sideways, putting some distance between them.

"Inherited what?" He watched her go with regret.

"The gift of persuasion. Just like your father and grandfather, you're confident in your ability to talk your way out of or into anything."

Caleb wasn't like his father or his grandfather. At least he didn't want to be like them. He tried very hard to mitigate his father's character traits in himself. For the most part, he thought he succeeded.

"That's not fair," he said.

"Fair?" She gave a light laugh. "A Watford talking about fair? Let me add to that. A Watford talking about fair while he tries to talk a Parker out of something?"

Caleb knew he'd lost this round. There was no way she was going to listen to reason. At least not right now. The kiss had been a colossal error.

Then again, it was a fantastic kiss. He couldn't bring himself to regret it. If that kiss was the biggest mistake he made today, it was going to be a good day.

"No comeback?" she asked. "Come on, Caleb. You're disappointing me."

"Is there anything I can say to change your opinion?"

"Uh, no."

"Then is there any chance you'll go out with me?"

The question seemed to take her aback, and it took her a second to respond. "You mean like on a date?"

"Yeah. You and me. Dinner, dancing, whatever." He wasn't exactly sure how they'd separate their personal attraction from their business interests, but he was more than willing to give it a try.

"Is that a joke? Are you trying to put me off balance?"

"Yes, I'm trying to put you off balance." He took a couple of steps toward her. "But no, it's not a joke. There's obviously an attraction between us."

"We have nothing in common."

"I like kissing you." And he was pretty confident that she liked kissing him.

Her expression didn't soften at all. "I bet you like kissing a whole lot of women."

Not as much as he liked kissing her. But the accusation was fundamentally true. And he didn't want to lie to her. "I suppose I do."

"Then take one of *them* out on a date."

"I'd rather take you."

"You're too much."

"You're stubborn."

"Give the man a gold star."

The answer surprised him. "You admit to being stubborn?"

"Oh, yes." She jabbed her finger against his chest. "And you ain't seen nothin' yet."

He trapped her hand, holding it against his heart. "Fightin' words?"

"You said it yourself. We're both going back to our corners now to come out swinging."

Her eyes were alight, her cheeks still flushed, her lips were still swollen from his kisses, and he could see a little pulse at the base of her neck. She was the sexiest woman on the planet.

"Don't you dare," she said, snatching her hand from his grip.

He couldn't help but grin. "I'm not going to kiss you again."

"You better not."

"I'll make you a deal."

She shook her head.

"Not a business deal. A personal deal. Next time, you have to be the one to kiss me." Even as he said the words, he feared he was making a mistake.

She might never decide to kiss him. But he had no choice. He couldn't take the chance of misreading her signals.

Melissa bounced through the doorway, enthusiasm in her expression and in her tone. "Jules, this is Noah Glover. He's offered to help us with the renovation."

Jules expression immediately neutralized, erasing their kiss, their argument and everything else. Noah Glover had walked in, and she'd given him a brilliant smile that made Caleb jealous.

Noah was tall and brawny, with an unshaven face and a shaggy haircut. He looked like the kind of guy who worked all day out in the weather.

Jules smoothly closed the space between them. "Nice to meet you, Noah."

They shook, and Caleb felt another shot of jealousy. He gave himself a ruthless shake. It was one thing to want to kiss her, even hold her, even strip her naked and make love to her—which he did. But it was something else altogether to be jealous of a man shaking her hand. He wasn't about to let that happen.

"I hope Melissa warned you we're on a tight budget," Jules said to Noah. "We want to do as much of the work as we can ourselves."

"I can work with a budget," Noah said. "And as much work as you're willing to do is fine with me."

"That sounds perfect." She was still shaking his hand.

That was it? The entire interview? They were going to hire the guy right here and now? What about reference checks?

Caleb stepped up and stuck out his own hand. "Caleb Watford. I'm a neighbor." He wanted this Noah guy to know he couldn't simply stride in and take advantage of Jules and Melissa.

"Nice to meet you," Noah said.

His grip was firm. Of course his grip was firm. He was a carpenter. But Caleb was no slouch. From what he could see, they were about the same height. Caleb could bench press one-eighty, but Noah had a lot more calluses.

"And our sworn enemy," Jules said.

Caleb slid her a look of annoyance. Did she have no idea that he was trying to help?

"What happened while I was gone?" Melissa asked, glancing from one to the other.

"Nothing," Jules said quickly. "Well, more of the same."

"I'm happy to get started tomorrow," Noah said to the women. "If you pull together your budget, I'll get going on some estimates, and we can see what we have for options."

His voice was deep. Caleb wasn't crazy to learn that. He'd heard women liked men with deep voices. It was supposed to instill a sense of confidence. He didn't want Jules feeling overconfident with this stranger.

Caleb had never heard of Noah Glover. Was he local to the Whiskey Bay area? Was he passing through? His truck outside was old and battered, and he wasn't exactly a poster child for professionalism. Caleb was definitely going to check him out.

"I'm up for that," Melissa said. "I'm excited to get started."

Noah gave her a nod. "Until tomorrow, then." He gave a parting smile to Jules before he left the building.

"He really seems to know what he's doing," Melissa said as she watched him leave.

"You just met him," Caleb said.

Both women looked at him in surprise.

"How can you judge his competency?" Caleb doubted either Jules or Melissa had any expertise in construction.

"He seemed open and straightforward," Melissa said. "Talked in plain language. He came highly recommended."

"Did you check his reviews?" Caleb asked.

"Melissa has a business degree," Jules said.

That was news to Caleb. He didn't know why it surprised him.

"Of course I checked his reviews," Melissa said. "I am aware of the internet."

Caleb wasn't sure whether to backpedal or press forward. "I only meant…"

Jules's voice turned to a sarcastic purr. "That sweet li'l young things like us might not know how to manage in the big bad world?"

He frowned at her. "I wondered why you'd trust him in a heartbeat and be so suspicious of me."

"Experience and good judgment," she said.

"That's not fair."

"I told you before, Caleb. You're a Watford. There isn't a reason in the world for me to be fair to you."

"He really is hot," Melissa said two days later.

Jules looked up from where she was stripping varnish from the wooden bar, expecting to see Caleb walk through the door. But he wasn't there. At least, she couldn't see him.

Melissa was pulling down the window trim, while Noah was outside setting up a survey level on a tripod.

Jules was momentarily confused and, she hated to admit, a little disappointed. Caleb might be annoying, but he was also interesting. He energized a room.

"You mean Noah?" she asked her sister.

"Who else would I mean? Look at those shoulders and those biceps."

"He does seem to be in good shape," Jules agreed.

She hadn't thought of Noah as particularly hot, although she supposed he was fairly good-looking in a rugged, earthy kind of way. He was dressed in a khaki green T-shirt and a pair of tan cargo pants. A tool belt was slung low on his hips, and his steel-toed boots were scuffed and worn. He had sandy-blond hair, thick and a little shaggy.

"I can't stop staring at him," Melissa said.

"I wouldn't have pegged him as your type."

The men Melissa had dated in college had been mostly preppy intellectuals, sometimes even poets. Occasionally, she'd talked about seeing an athlete. There was one basketball player she'd stayed with for a couple of months.

"Hot and sexy? Whose type is that not?"

Jules smiled, taking another look at Noah through her safety glasses. "So you mean as eye candy."

Personally, she found him a bit dusty for eye candy. But if Melissa found him entertaining while she took on the drudge work of renovating, Jules was happy for her.

"Don't let him slow you down," Jules said.

"I can look and rip trim at the same time."

"Make sure you don't stab yourself with a nail."

"They're finishing nails, teeny-tiny finishing nails. Do you think if it gets hot enough he'll consider taking off his shirt?"

"I think if you ask him we get sued. Sexual harassment goes both ways, you know."

"I won't ask him, at least, not flat out."

"You can't ask him at all. You can't even hint."

"I can hope."

"I suppose there's no such thing as the mind police," Jules said.

Melissa grinned. "That's a good thing. Because what I'm imagining is probably illegal in most states."

"Please don't tell me."

"You're such a prude."

Jules scrunched her eyes shut, not allowing any untoward mental pictures to form. "Pink fuzzy bunnies.

Pink fuzzy bunnies," she chanted out loud, bringing the harmless image into her mind.

Melissa laughed at her antics.

"I obviously missed something." This time it *was* Caleb.

Jules popped open her eyes to find him standing in the doorway again.

Talk about hot and sexy. He wore blue jeans, an open-collar white shirt and a midnight blue blazer. He looked casual and classy all at the same time, putting the rest of the male world to shame.

"Pink fuzzy bunnies?" he asked with a raised brow.

"Inside joke," Melissa said. "It's our mantra to keep nasty images at bay."

Caleb glanced around. "Is there something nasty?"

"Not *at all*," Melissa said, her blue eyes flashing mischief before she looked out the window again.

Jules told herself to stop ogling Caleb. "Can we help you with something?"

"I've been doing some research on your project," he said as he stepped inside.

She adjusted her gloves and went determinedly back to working on the varnish removal with a paint scraper. "You're just the Energizer Bunny, aren't you?"

He kept moving toward her. "You've obviously got a rabbit theme going here."

"Stay back," she warned. "This stuff is dangerous."

He stopped but frowned. "Do you know what you're doing?"

"Yes." She dug the blade into the tacky solution and scraped it off in a layer.

"Have you done this before?"

"I watched a YouTube video." She wiped away the goo with a rag and started on another strip.

"So, your answer is no."

"My answer is 'it's none of your business.'"

He seemed to find her response amusing. "You're very prickly."

"And you're a cocklebur."

"A what?"

"A prickly plant. Something that digs in and sticks to you and won't let go."

"Oh. Okay, my mind went to a completely different place with that."

Jules struggled not to smile. She didn't want to encourage him. Or maybe she did. She didn't like that he felt so free to interfere in her life, but she'd admit he was at least as entertaining for her as Noah was for Melissa.

A low clatter sounded from the window where Melissa was working. She swore.

Jules quickly glanced up. "You okay?"

Caleb was there before Melissa could answer, removing an L-shaped piece of window trim from her hands and untangling another piece from around her feet. "Are you hurt?"

"I'm fine," Melissa said. "I just got distracted for a minute."

"Where are you putting all this?" Caleb asked.

"There's a disposal bin in the parking lot."

Caleb spotted a pair of work gloves in a box by the door. He helped himself and gathered up a full armload of discarded trim.

"You're not dressed for work," Jules felt the need to point out to him.

"Not exactly," he agreed. "But I might as well help a bit while we talk."

"We're not done talking?"

He didn't answer, just shook his head as he left through the door.

"You're as bad as me," Melissa said.

Jules realized she was watching Caleb's backside as he walked away. "Is it that obvious?"

"It is when you start drooling."

"You're *such* a comedian. I'm trying to figure out what he's doing here."

"That's not what your expression says. But, okay, let's go with that. What do you suppose he's doing here?"

"He said he'd done some research on our project."

"What does that mean?" Melissa asked.

"I'm assuming more on why we should remove the noncompete clause."

"That seems likely. He's coming back."

"I see that."

Caleb gave Noah a curt nod of acknowledgment as he approached the restaurant doorway.

Jules found the view of him equally pleasant from the front. She didn't have to like him to admire the breadth of his shoulders, the swing of his stride, and the square chin and neatly trimmed dark hair that made him look capable of taking on...well, anything, including her.

A wave of heat passed through her body and sweat tickled her forehead. She swiped awkwardly at her hairline with her bare forearm as he walked back inside.

He looked around the open space. "What else needs doing?"

"Your work is done," Jules said.

He might be pleasant to watch, but she was coming to the conclusion that it might be dangerous for her to spend much time around him.

He removed his jacket and set it aside, rolling up his sleeves.

"You have got to be kidding me," she said. "You're going to ruin that shirt."

He shrugged. "I have other shirts."

"It's *white*."

He glanced down at himself. "So it is."

"Say whatever it is you came to say, and get out of here. Go back to your regularly scheduled life."

He put a mock expression of hurt on his face. "I don't know how to take that."

"Yes, you do. You've got your own construction project to worry about."

"That's the thing."

"Here we go..." She lined up to scrape off another strip of varnish.

"I want to show you some of the numbers from my other Neo locations."

Out of the corner of her eye, she watched him look into their small toolbox. "Showing off your profits?" she asked.

He ignored her gibe. "And the plans for the new location." He selected a claw hammer. "What's your seating going to be here?"

"None of your business."

"Jules." There was exaggerated patience in his tone. "We're not going to be able to work this out if you're going to be hostile."

Melissa spoke up. "Thirty-four at the tables, twelve at the bar and another eighteen on the deck."

Jules glared at her.

"What?" Melissa asked. "It's not exactly a state secret. All he has to do is pull a copy of the business license."

"Neo will have one-seventy-two on two floors, plus fifty seasonally on the patio. We're not your competition." He approached the window opposite Melissa and wedged the hammer under the trim.

"I agree with that," Jules said. "It would be no contest at all."

"Why would anyone choose the Crab Shack?" Melissa asked.

"They wouldn't," Jules said.

"Because they love seafood. And because nobody wants to eat at the same place all the time. And because if they came to Neo, they'd see the Crab Shack and maybe become curious."

"Or maybe they'd come to the Crab Shack and learn about Neo." Jules didn't know why she tossed that out. It sounded ridiculous even to her.

"Sure," Caleb said.

"Don't patronize me. We both know that's not going to happen. What you're offering us is your leftovers."

"Neo is a nationally recognized chain with international awards and a substantial marketing program. I'm not going to apologize for that."

"Fancy it up all you want, but the result will be the same. Neo wins, the Crab Shack loses. We're far better off being the only option at Whiskey Bay."

"Can I at least show you my floor plans?"

"Sure," Melissa said.

*"Melissa."*

"What's the harm in looking, Jules? Aren't you even a little bit curious?"

Jules was, but there was no way she'd admit it. "Go ahead and look if you want. I'm not interested."

"I'll bring them by later on," Caleb said as he ripped down a long strip of window trim.

"He is *not* changing our minds." Jules put complete conviction into her tone, even as she struggled to drag her gaze from Caleb.

Due to the curve of the shoreline, Caleb could see the Neo construction site through the window of his great room. He could also see the Crab Shack, where lights were on tonight. And he could see the Parkers' house—all dark there.

"Jules wouldn't even look at the plans," he said turning back to his lawyer, Bernard Stackhouse.

"What did you expect?" Bernard asked in an even tone.

"I thought she might look. I hoped she'd look. I hoped she'd see reason and stop being so stubborn."

"And then do things your way?"

Bernard was sitting in one of Caleb's leather armchairs. His suit was impeccable as always, and he looked distinguished with a touch of gray at his temples. He could flare into passion in a courtroom when the need arose, but Caleb knew it was an act. He wasn't sure Bernard even felt emotions. But the man wasn't shy about using sarcasm.

"I absolutely want her to do things my way."

His way was the closest they could get to a win-win. But Jules wouldn't take that. She wouldn't even consider it. She insisted on going for a win-lose.

"Her sister, Melissa, seems a whole lot more reasonable," he said.

"Can she change Jules's mind?"

"I'm not sure she's trying. But she did like my restaurant plans." Caleb's gaze was drawn back to the still, silent darkness of his construction site.

He could picture the finished building in his mind, the exterior, the interior, all the people they'd employ and the happy diners enjoying the picturesque waterfront. He was growing more and more impatient to get there. Every day he had to wait he couldn't help calculating the cost: the leased equipment, the crew on standby, the delay in opening that was going to cost him money. If this had to end in a win-lose, he wanted to make sure it wasn't him on the crappy end of the deal.

"I did find an interesting new option," Bernard said.

Caleb turned. "And you're just speaking up now?"

"I thought you wanted to vent."

"I did want to vent. But I want a solution a whole lot more."

"Why don't you sit down?" Bernard asked.

"Exactly what kind of an option is it?" Was it so shocking that Caleb couldn't be trusted to keep his feet?

"My neck's getting sore from looking up at you. Sit down."

Caleb thought better on his feet. But he was curious enough to go along. He perched on the arm of the sofa.

"You look like a coiled spring," Bernard said.

"You drawing this out won't make me less coiled."

"This isn't a five-second explanation."

"I hope not, because you've already used up two minutes in the preamble."

Bernard smiled. "You're a lot like your father."

"You're just going to pile it on, aren't you?"

"There's an easement," Bernard said.

Caleb heard the side door to his house swing open. He knew it would either be Matt or TJ.

"In here," he called out.

"Do you want me to wait until we're alone?" Bernard asked.

"Why would I want that? Is it a secret option? Is it illegal?"

"Is what illegal?" Matt asked as he strolled into the room.

"Yes," Bernard drawled. "As your lawyer, I feel it's my duty to advise you to break the law."

"That's a first," Matt said, taking another armchair. "What are we drinking?"

"I'm considering tequila," Caleb said.

Matt rose again and headed for the bar.

"Keep talking," Caleb prompted Bernard.

Bernard exhaled an exaggerated sigh of impatience, like he was the one who'd been kept waiting.

"There's an easement," he repeated, producing a map from his briefcase and unfolding it on the coffee table between them. "The access road for the Crab Shack crosses your land." He pointed. "Right here."

"You mean TJ's land."

"No. All four residential lots were originally a single parcel. TJ's, Matt's and the Parkers' lots were carved out at minimum size, and the remainder stayed with the parcel your grandfather purchased. The effect is a peninsula of land owned by you that runs in front of each of the other properties. Nobody pays attention to it, because it's mostly the sheer face of a cliff. That is, except for the access road."

Caleb leaned forward to study the map lines.

Matt returned with three glasses of tequila.

"I thought you'd know I was joking," Caleb said to Matt. He'd expected Matt to open a few beers.

"Too late now."

Caleb wasn't a big tequila fan, but he accepted the glass anyway.

If he was reading the map correctly, where the Crab Shack driveway branched off the access road, it crossed his land for about two hundred yards.

"On one side of the driveway is a cliff," Bernard said.

Matt crouched on one knee. "And the other is too close to the high water mark. It's vulnerable to tidal surges if there's a storm."

"Is it possible for her to reroute along the shore?" Caleb asked.

"I talked to an engineer," Bernard said. "In effect, she'd have to build a bridge."

"They're on a budget."

"Then, there's your answer."

Matt gave a whistle. "That's playin' hardball."

"I'm losing ten thousand a day in idle equipment rental."

"So, you'd bankrupt her?"

"I'd use it for leverage." Caleb straightened to contemplate.

He'd already tried the carrot. Maybe it was time for the stick. He'd show Jules that if they didn't work together, it would mean mutual assured annihilation. Surely she couldn't be so stubborn as to choose that option.

Caleb's front door opened again, and TJ strode in from the hall. "We ready to go?" There was an eagerness in his tone.

The three men had agreed to hit a club in Olympia tonight. It had seemed like a good idea at the time. But now Caleb was regretting the commitment. He'd rather stay home. He didn't plan to confront Jules with the threat of canceling her easement tonight, but he wasn't in the mood for dancing and inconsequential conversation with random women either.

"Is that an ambulance?" TJ asked, gazing out the window.

Caleb turned as he stood, immediately seeing the flashing lights closing in on the Crab Shack.

"That's not good," Matt said, rising to his feet.

Caleb was already heading for the door, with Matt and TJ at his heels.

The fastest way to the Crab Shack was along the footpath. Caleb broke into a run. He knew every inch of the pathway, and it took him less than five minutes to get to the peninsula, his mind going over all the possible scenarios where Jules might have been hurt. Had she fallen off the ladder? Had she burned herself with the paint stripper?

Matt stuck with him, with TJ falling a bit behind. Caleb had no idea whether or not Bernard had even bothered to come along. As he ran up the gravel driveway, he could see the paramedics moving a stretcher. He put on a burst of speed.

Then he saw Jules under the lights. She wasn't the one on the stretcher. He felt an immense surge of relief. But then his fear was back. If it wasn't Jules, it must be Melissa.

He finally got close enough to call out.

"What happened?" he asked.

Jules looked over at him in surprise. "What are you doing here?"

"We saw the ambulance lights," he said through the gasps of his breath. "What happened?"

"Nail gun," Melissa said from the stretcher, her voice sounding strained.

Caleb was relieved to hear her speak. But then her words registered.

"You were using a nail gun?" He moved his attention to Jules. "You have a *nail gun*?"

"*I* don't have a nail gun. Noah has a nail gun."

"Where's Noah?" Caleb wanted to have a word with the man. What was he thinking letting Jules and Melissa use a nail gun? Was he crazy?

"It was my fault," Melissa called from inside the ambulance.

"Are you coming with us?" the paramedic asked Jules.

"Yes." She moved for the door.

"I'll meet you there," Caleb said.

"Why?" she asked as she stepped up to climb inside.

"Just go."

"Melissa seemed pretty good," Matt said.

TJ arrived, panting.

"You need to hit the gym," Matt told him.

"No kidding," TJ said. "Who got hurt?"

"Melissa," Caleb said. "Something about a nail gun."

TJ gave him an incredulous look. "Is it bad?"

"She was talking from the stretcher. But I'm going to head down to Memorial and find out what happened."

"You are?" TJ seemed surprised.

Caleb thought it was a perfectly reasonable course of action. The women were their neighbors, and Jules might need something. At the very least, she'd need a ride back home.

"White knight syndrome," Matt said.

"Who's he rescuing?" TJ asked.

"Good question." TJ raised a brow at Caleb. "The rational one or the difficult one?"

*The difficult one.* "Neither."

Caleb was simply being neighborly…and practical. He was being neighborly and practical. There was nothing remotely unusual about that.

# Three

Jules couldn't decide whether to sit down and wait patiently for news or to pace the hospital waiting room floor and worry. Melissa had seemed okay in the ambulance, in surprisingly good spirits considering she had a large nail protruding through the middle of her left hand. Jules had assumed her sister couldn't have been too badly hurt if she was awake and joking. But she might have been in shock. She could quite easily have been in shock.

Opting for pacing, Jules walked the hall then turned at the narrow, vinyl sofa and walked back toward the vending machines. If Melissa was in shock, then the pain might not have been registering. She could be really hurt. The hospital staff had certainly taken the injury seriously, whisking her off to a trauma room. Jules had tried to follow, but the nurse had urged her to stay out of the way and let the medical staff do their work.

When Jules turned again, she saw Caleb at the end of the hallway walking swiftly toward her. He looked tall, broad-shouldered and capable, and she felt an inexplicable sense of relief at the sight of him. As soon as the feeling registered, she banished it. It was embarrassing to react that way. He wasn't a medical professional. He wasn't a friend. He wasn't a significant person in either her or Melissa's life. There was no reason his presence should be comforting, none at all.

"Is Melissa all right?" he asked as he approached, concern clear in his tone.

She felt an inexcusable urge to walk straight into his arms. She wouldn't do it, of course, but a little part of her couldn't help wondering how he'd react if she did.

"They've taken her into surgery."

He frowned as he came to a halt. "That sounds concerning."

"They told me it was a precaution."

His intense look of interest prompted her to continue.

"There's a hand specialist in the hospital tonight, and he wants to be sure they don't damage any nerves or tendons taking out the nail. At least that's what they said." She had to fight the urge to lean on him again. "You don't think they'd downplay it, do you?"

"Are you worried?" he asked, moving slightly closer.

She wished he'd keep his distance. It was easier to resist him that way.

"No. I can't decide. Should I be worried? The truth is I'm worried that I'm not worried. Does that make sense?"

"Yes."

"She was still talking when we arrived. I thought that was a good sign. But now I'm thinking she might have been in shock."

"I suppose that's possible." He looked thoughtful.

"You could have just said it was a good sign."

He gave a slight smile. "I think it was a good sign."

"Too late."

"I suppose." He paused. "But it was probably a good sign."

"Noble effort."

"I don't see why they'd downplay it for you. They'd want you to be prepared for any bad news."

"Okay. I'll give you that one." Jules relaxed a little. She moved and sat down on a padded chair.

Caleb followed, taking a chair across from her. They were both silent for a few moments.

It was Caleb who broke it. "Do you know what was she doing with the nail gun?"

"She was showing me how it worked. Noah had shown her earlier. And, well, it went off. We didn't expect that."

An expression of annoyance crossed Caleb's face. "Noah showed her how to use a nail gun?"

"It's not Noah's fault."

"What was he thinking?"

"That she asked a question and he answered it."

"I don't mean to sound sexist—"

Jules felt her spine stiffen. "But you're about to."

"I guess I am. Are you sure that the two of you should be undertaking a construction project?"

"We're not undertaking a construction project. We're helping with a construction project. Noah has been great about showing us what to do and how to do it."

Caleb frowned again. "He didn't do so well with the nail gun."

"Ms. Parker?" A nurse interrupted.

Jules immediately switched her attention. "You have news?" She came to her feet.

Caleb rose with her.

The smile on the nurse's face was encouraging, but it seemed to take forever for her to speak. "Your sister is out of surgery. It went very well."

"Thank you," Jules whispered, relief rushing through her. She realized then just how frightened she'd been.

"She's in recovery for the next hour or so, and then she'll likely sleep through the night. There's no need for you to stay."

"So her hand will be fine?"

"The surgeon is anticipating a complete recovery. She'll need to rest it for a couple of weeks. She can follow up with her family doctor."

"We're new in town. We don't have—"

"She can see my doctor," Caleb put in. His hand went to the small of Jules's back and rested lightly there.

She looked skeptically up at him. Good doctors had been difficult to find in Portland. Most had closed practices and weren't taking new patients.

"He'll see her." Caleb spoke with authority, seeming to guess Jules's hesitation.

She was reminded of his wealth, and the power it likely brought him. She realized his doctor would probably grant any favor Caleb asked. Her first reaction was to refuse on principle. But Melissa's health was at stake, and Jules knew she couldn't let pride stand in the way of the best care for her.

"Thank you," she said instead.

Caleb smiled, and his hand firmed against her back. Warmth and pleasure flowed through her before she remembered to shut it down.

"Can I see Melissa?" Jules asked the nurse.

"Not for at least an hour. She's in recovery." The nurse's gaze went to the clock on the wall, which showed that it was well past midnight.

"You might as well come back in the morning," Caleb said. "You need some sleep, too."

Again, Jules wanted to argue with him on principle. But she was tired, and he wasn't wrong, especially if Melissa was only going to sleep anyway.

"I'll drive you home," he said, seeming to take her silence for agreement.

It was, but that didn't mean she wanted him to make the assumption. But now wasn't the time to make an issue of it.

She directed her attention to the nurse instead, reaching out to squeeze the woman's hands in gratitude. "Thank you so much. Will you thank the surgeon for me?"

"I will."

The nurse departed, and Jules stepped away from Caleb's touch as they walked down the corridor.

"I can get a cab," she said as they approached the double doors of the foyer.

"Sure you could," he said. "And that makes perfect sense. Especially since I'm driving past your house on my way home."

"We're not your responsibility," she felt compelled to point out.

He pushed open the door. "Nobody said you were."

"What are you doing here anyway?" The night wind was brisk against her thin T-shirt, and she wrapped her arms around herself.

"I wanted to make sure Melissa was okay. And I knew you'd need a ride home."

"You barely know us."

He indicated a black Lexus parked near the door. "I've known you for twenty-four years."

"You've disliked me for twenty-four years. It's not the same thing."

"I never disliked you." Something softened in his tone. "I barely knew you."

"You dislike me now."

"I'm annoyed with you right now. That's not the same thing either."

"Close enough."

He cracked a smile as he opened the passenger door. "You do make it difficult to like you, Jules."

"Because I won't give in and give you what you want."

"That's part of it." He closed the door and crossed to the driver's side.

"What's the other part?" she asked as he took his seat and pressed the starter button.

To her relief, warm air immediately blew through the dashboard vents.

"You disagree with virtually everything I say."

She thought about that. "Not with everything you say."

He gave an ironic shake of his head, but he smiled again, too.

She liked his smile. She had to stop liking his smile. And his touch, she really had to stop liking his touch.

He pulled out of the parking spot and headed for the winding coastal road back to their houses. "Name one thing where you've agreed with me."

"I'm letting you drive me home."

"I had to talk you into that."

"Proving I can change my mind," she said with triumph. "I'm a reasonable person who can change her mind when presented with evidence."

"In that case, let me explain about how…"

Her heart sank a bit. "Not tonight, Caleb."

"I was joking."

She suddenly felt drained of energy and realized she'd been running on adrenaline since the accident, and the relief that had buoyed her at learning Melissa would recover had already worn off. Now she was just exhausted.

"Are you hungry?" he surprised her by asking.

She was, but she didn't want to admit it. It felt like she'd be showing him another weakness.

"I'm starving," he said. "Do you mind if we stop?"

"You're driving. It's your car. You can do whatever you like."

He glanced her way. "Have I done something to annoy you just now?"

She instantly felt guilty. "No." That was a lie. "Yes." That wasn't quite right either. "I wish you'd quit being nice. It makes me nervous."

He laughed, and the rich sound was somehow soothing to her nerves.

He took an abrupt left, entering the parking lot of a fast-food place. "Burger okay with you?"

"Whatever you're having," she said. She was hungry, not fussy.

He pulled up to the drive-through window, and a young woman slid back the glass.

Considering the late hour, the girl's smile was positively perky. "What can I get for you?"

"Two cheeseburgers, two fries and two chocolate shakes," Caleb said.

She rang up the order, and Caleb handed her some bills.

"Coming right up." She pulled back, the smile still in place.

"Comfort food," Jules said, thinking it fit the circumstances.

"I forgot you were a chef."

"I wasn't being critical."

"You weren't?"

She gave him an eye roll. "If you're going to jump to conclusions, you should learn to interpret my intonation."

"I thought that was sarcasm."

"It wasn't. I've got nothing against burgers and fries. They get a bad rap. They're tasty. Okay, maybe not so nutritious as to be a daily recommendation. But I'm not really in the mood for nutrition right now."

He smiled and seemed to relax. They both fell silent.

"Thanks for this," she said a few minutes later.

"Not a problem."

The window opened and the girl handed Caleb his change and the food.

He set the milk shakes in the console between them and passed the warm, fragrant paper bag to Jules. Then he pulled across the shoreline road into a parking lot overlooking the ocean. He shut off the engine and released his seat belt.

"This okay?" he asked her.

"Perfect." She released her own seat belt and sat back in the comfy leather seat, letting the tension of the past few hours drain from her.

Melissa was going to be okay. Everything else would work itself out around that.

Caleb relieved her of the bag and handed back a burger wrapped in waxed paper, and then a small carton of fries. She popped one of the fries in her mouth. It was crisp and flavorful, salty and satisfying.

"Mmm," she said.

He smiled and gave a small shake of his head. "You're awfully easy to please."

"My needs are simple." She took the closest milk shake and drew the cold, creamy liquid through the straw.

"You surprise me, Juliet Parker."

"You should be the one surprising me by appreciating burgers."

"Why is that?"

"I'm an ordinary Portland girl. You're a successful millionaire who lives in a mansion on the hill."

"I suppose that's true," he agreed, a trace of laughter in his voice.

She unfolded the wrapper, pulling it away from the sticky cheese. "If anyone should be snobby about fast food, it's you."

"I normally add a garnish of caviar."

"Now, *that's* more what I expected."

"Then I'm likely to keep surprising you."

"Is this your pitch for being an ordinary guy?"

"I am an ordinary guy."

"You own seventeen restaurants."

"You did some research."

"I did," she admitted. "I've concluded you don't need an eighteenth."

He paused. "You really want to have that argument now?"

She didn't. She wasn't sure why she'd brought it up. Or maybe she was. They were getting along, and that made her nervous. She'd wanted to remind herself of what stood between them. She didn't want to like Caleb. She didn't dare.

The burgers finished and the drive complete, Caleb stepped out of his car at the top of the stairs that led down to the Parker house.

"What are you doing?" Suspicion was clear in Jules's tone as she closed the passenger door behind her.

"I'm walking you to your door." He came around to meet up with her at the edge of the gravel driveway where the long staircase took off for the house below.

"Don't be silly."

"I'm never silly."

"I'm perfectly capable of walking down my own front steps. I've done it a thousand times."

"Maybe so." He gestured for her to go first. "But I'm incapable of leaving a woman on her dark doorstep and hoping for the best."

*"Caleb."* Her exasperation was clear.

"Give it up, Jules. I'm walking you to your door. My old man might not have done much right, but he did raise me to be a gentleman."

"This is senseless." But she started to move.

"Maybe. But it's not going to hurt anything either. You really do need to learn to pick your battles."

"And you need to learn how to deploy your energy."

He smiled to himself as he followed her down. He was perfectly happy with his deployment of energy. He had a feeling he'd walk miles just to keep arguing with her.

The wooden steps felt punky beneath his feet, springing slightly with his weight. Squinting, he could make out what looked like moss growing at the edges.

"How old is this staircase?" he asked.

"I have no idea."

He gave the rail a pointed wiggle. "It needs to be replaced."

"I'll get right on it."

"I'm serious, Jules. This could be dangerous."

Forget the possibility of it giving way, the aging wood was slimy and slippery. Somebody was going to fall, and it was a long, long way down. He peered at the dim, distant porchlight.

"It's none of your concern, Caleb. And there are a lot of pressing issues in my life right now, including an injured sister."

He immediately felt like a heel. "I'm sorry."

He wished he'd gone first. That way, if she slipped in the dark, she'd have him to break her fall. He should have thought of that. Why hadn't he thought of that?

As a stopgap measure, he reached for her hand, enveloping it in his, thinking he could at least brace her if she slipped.

She tried to tug her hand away.

He was having none of it. "Pick your battles," he reminded her.

"This isn't a date," she tossed over her shoulder.

"I sure hope not." The idea was downright alarming. "Fast food and a trip to the emergency room? That would be the worst date in the world."

"To be clear, this little walk to the door, holding my hand, cozying up. You're not getting a kiss good-night."

"I'm holding your hand to keep you from falling."

"Of course you are." The sarcasm was back.

"You're a very suspicious woman."

"You're a very calculating man."

"I'm not angling for a kiss." Though he'd be lying if he pretended he didn't want one. "But, just for the sake of argument, what would it take? Exactly how good would the date have to be for a guy to get a kiss from you?"

"It has nothing to do with the quality of the date. I mean, of course, it would have to be a good date. By that I mean an enjoyable date. But it wouldn't have to be an expensive date. I'm not about to be bowled over by opulent surroundings and fine wine."

"Cheap wine it is."

They'd reached her porch, and she turned. "It's the caliber of the company that counts."

She was beautiful in the starlight.

"I've been told I'm a good conversationalist," he noted.

"I bet you have. And I bet it was by women who were enjoying fine wine and opulent surroundings?"

"You have a low opinion of your own gender, Juliet."

His response seemed to throw her, and her brow furrowed.

"I didn't mean it that way," she said.

"I know how you meant it. You think I date women who like me for my money."

"Not exactly..."

He had her off balance, and he took advantage of it, easing forward. "I don't believe this. You've actually talked yourself into a corner."

"No, I haven't. Just give me a second."

"Sure." He waited, enjoying the view of her blue eyes, pupils overlarge in the dim light, shining like windows to her soul.

"This isn't fair," she finally said in a husky voice.

"Why not?"

"I'm tired. I'm not at my best."

"You need me to give you a head start?"

It was clear she had to fight a grin.

"You know what your problem is?" he asked, brushing the back of his hand softly against her cheek.

He expected her to pull back, but she didn't.

"What is my problem?" Her voice was suddenly breathy.

"You don't know what to do about me."

She paused, and her white teeth scraped across her bottom lip. "I wish I could argue with that—"

"But you're tired," he finished the sentence for her. "And you're not at your best."

His gaze and his mind fixated on her lips. He wanted very badly to kiss them.

"I'm tired," she agreed and seemed to sway toward him. "And I'm not at my best."

He cupped his other palm over her shoulder. "Jules."

Her blue eyes clouded, and her lips parted. She seemed unfocused as she gazed up at him. "Yes."

His voice was husky to his own ears. "Do you want me to kiss you?"

"Yes." Then she seemed to realize what she'd revealed. "I mean—"

If she was about to change her answer, she was too late. She'd said yes. He'd heard it loud and clear.

Their kiss was better than he remembered, even better than his imagination. Her lips were tender and hot. She tasted sweet. And when he probed with his tongue, she answered in kind, tipping her head and leaning against him.

Her body was soft and warm, her curves smooth

against his angles. He wrapped his arms around her, enveloping her while the kiss went on. Arousal throbbed deep and hard within him, and his mind galloped ahead to an image of a soft bed, with her naked body entwined around his.

Why couldn't it always be like this? Why did they have to fight? She was smart and sassy, and probably the most interesting woman he'd ever met. She was certainly the most exciting.

And then reality slammed into him.

They did have to fight. And no amount of wishing would change that.

His interests were diametrically opposed to hers. He probably had to hurt her. He had no choice. And if he was going to hurt her, he shouldn't be kissing her. He absolutely couldn't sleep with her—not with the secret he was keeping right now.

He pulled back, breaking the kiss.

She all but staggered in shock. "What—"

"I'm sorry," he said, reluctantly letting his arms drop away from her. "That was out of line."

She still seemed to be getting her bearings. "Uh, okay."

"It's late. You're tired," he repeated the words, forcing himself to keep talking. "This wasn't a date, and I shouldn't be so presumptuous."

"You did ask permission," she pointed out.

He couldn't believe she was arguing his side. "And you were about to change your answer. I knew that. I could tell."

"I was weighing the pros and cons."

"There are a lot of cons." That at least was the truth.

Her gaze was opaque and welcoming. "There are a lot of pros."

"Don't do that, Jules."

"Don't do what?"

"Don't give me permission."

"But—"

"Tomorrow we'll be fighting again. I can guarantee it."

She offered a small smile. "We're not fighting now."

Caleb gritted his teeth. If he didn't walk away right now, he wouldn't walk away at all.

"Good night, Jules." He told his feet to move.

She took a staggering step back. "Wow. Talk about hot and cold."

His brain echoed her tone of incredulity. He couldn't explain it to her, but he felt like he'd been doused with ice water. "I'll set it up with the doctor. Let me know if there's anything else Melissa needs."

Jules didn't respond. She just blinked in obvious confusion.

He finally forced his feet to move, turning away from temptation before he did something they'd both massively regret.

The next day, Jules struggled to keep Caleb's kiss from her mind. She'd picked Melissa up from the hospital and tried to convince her to rest at home. But Melissa insisted on coming with Jules to the Crab Shack.

As they walked in the door, Noah took in her bandaged hand. His gaze went immediately to where they had discarded the nail gun before swinging back to zero in on Melissa's face.

"*What* did I tell you?" he asked her pointedly.

"Not to touch—"

"*What* did you do?" He advanced on her.

"I was only—"

"Only what? Only *what*?" Noah's shoulders were squared, his voice harsher than normal.

"She was showing me how it worked," Jules put in, surprised by Noah's strong reaction. He was normally easygoing and totally restrained.

Noah turned his head to give Jules a look of disbelief. "Can I speak with your sister alone?"

"Not if you're going to yell at her."

"I'm not yelling."

"He's not yelling," Melissa said, resignation in her tone.

"She was at the hospital last night," Jules told Noah. "They had to do surgery."

Noah's expression immediately turned to concern. He flipped his attention back to Melissa. "Are you all right? No permanent damage, right?"

"I'm fine," Melissa said. "They only kept me overnight—"

"They kept you *overnight*?"

"Just because of the anesthetic. I was sleeping."

He gently took hold of her forearm and lifted her injured hand to look at it from a few angles. "You're not allowed to touch anything."

"I get it. I won't."

"Ever again," he added. "None of my tools. None of any tools. I don't want you hammering or sawing."

"Noah," Jules interrupted, realizing he was going overboard.

"Painting?" Melissa asked with a little tease in her tone.

"Fumes," Noah said.

"I'll wear a mask."

"You need a helmet and body armor."

"Oh, come on. I'm not that bad."

He gazed pointedly at her bandaged hand. "Yes, you are."

Jules realized the tone of the argument had changed. He wasn't angry. They seemed to be having fun.

"Well, I'm not doing all the work myself," she put in lightly. "I don't mind keeping Melissa away from sharp objects."

"And heavy and hard objects, too," Noah said with a glance Jules's way.

"But she has to be able to help. We need her contribution."

He returned his attention to Melissa. "Painting is okay."

"I'm not sure who put you in charge of the project."

"I'm a skilled professional with industrial safety training. Have you had industrial safety training? When you can produce a certificate that says you have, you can be in charge of the jobsite."

Caleb's voice interrupted from the doorway, tight and demanding. "You let her use your nail gun?"

The memories of last night flooded back to Jules. Her skin heated up, and she swore she could smell Caleb's woodsy scent.

Noah clamped his jaw shut, and his gaze darkened on Caleb. "She wanted to see how it worked."

"And you showed her?" Caleb asked Noah.

"I told her not to touch it without me."

"That didn't work out so well, did it?"

Melissa spoke up, "It was my fault, Caleb, not Noah's."

"But you're the one who got hurt," Caleb said to her. "How are you? Should you even be here today?"

"She insisted," Jules said, finally finding her voice.

Whatever had happened, or not happened, between her and Caleb last night, it was over. She needed to forget about it and move on. Though she'd spent most of the night restless and disappointed, he'd been right. They were on opposite sides of a fight, and that fact wasn't about to change.

"Melissa is going to sit down," Noah said.

He still had hold of her forearm, and he led her across the restaurant.

Caleb moved closer to Jules, and her reaction to him intensified. She didn't want to be attracted to him, but she couldn't seem to turn it off. *Logic*, she told herself. If she used logic and reason, and remembered who he was and what he wanted from her, she'd be fine.

She braced herself.

"Can we talk?" he asked.

"About what?"

The last thing she needed was an intimate little re-hash of last night. He'd had his chance. He didn't take it. And she was glad of that. At least she would be glad of that, once her logic and reason kicked in.

"Business," he said, surprising her.

"Oh."

His expression tightened, and his nostrils flared ever so slightly.

"Sure," she said, making to follow Melissa across the room.

"Just you," Caleb said, keeping his voice low.

"What's going on, Caleb?"

"I don't want to upset her."

"But you're willing to upset me?"

A beat went by before he answered. "There's something you need to know."

She gave up trying to guess what he was getting at. "Sure. Fine. Out on the deck?"

"That'll work." He turned for the door.

She followed, out into the sunny June afternoon. Seagulls swooped through the salt-tang that hung in the air. The tide was high, waves battering the rocky shore, sending spray into the air and roaring softly in rhythm.

"Talk," Jules said, widening her stance and tipping up her chin.

Caleb halted at the rail and turned. "I've been talking to my lawyer."

"You can't sue us."

"I'm not going to sue you. Sue you for what? Why would I sue you?"

"I don't know. What else do lawyers do?"

Her comeback seemed to stump him for a moment.

"Defend criminals," he suggested.

"Have you committed a crime?"

"Of *course* not."

"Then why do you need a lawyer?"

He reached behind himself and braced a hand on the wooden rail. "He's a corporate lawyer."

"So you're dissolving the Whiskey Bay Neo location." She knew it was a long shot, but she figured she might as well go for the brass ring.

Caleb gave her a crooked frown. It was kind of endearing. No, no, no. She didn't want him to be endearing.

"My lawyer was looking at the land survey of your property."

"You can't have my land, Caleb."

"I don't want your land. Okay, I'd take your land if you didn't want it. Would you sell it to me?"

"And then I couldn't build the Crab Shack."

"Brilliant deduction."

"Don't get all superior on me."

"I'm not superior. I'm trying to tell you something."

"Then spit it out. Put some nouns and verbs together that make sense."

"I would if you'd be quiet for a minute."

Jules might not like his hostility. But her keeping quiet was the only way he could tell her what was on his mind. She made a show of zipping her lips shut. Then she folded her arms across her chest and waited.

Caleb's chest rose and fell with a deep breath. "There's no easy way to say this."

"I'm getting that impression," she muttered.

"I thought your lips were zipped."

She rezipped them.

"You have an easement. It's for your access road, and it goes across my land." He looked toward the shore, and she followed the direction of his gaze. "If I revoke the easement, nobody can get to the Crab Shack."

It took a minute for his words to penetrate.

When they did, she couldn't accept them. What he was saying didn't make sense.

"No," she said simply.

He had to be lying.

"It would take me a while to give you all the details," he said. "But it is the truth."

"I want the details."

He reached for his inside pocket and handed her an envelope. "This isn't a bluff."

"It can't possibly be true."

"Stroke of a pen, Jules. It's my land, and I can revoke your rights. Even if you build the Crab Shack, nobody will be able to come."

She felt the world shift beneath her. "You wouldn't."

"I don't want to."

"It can't be legal. I'm getting my own lawyer."

"That's your choice."

"You bet it's my choice." Like he could stop her.

"But I'd rather we worked together and made both places a success." He looked completely unfazed by her threat.

"You think you can scare me into removing the noncompete clause." She tilted forward, trying to look tough.

"I'm not trying to scare you. I'm attempting to appeal to your sense of reason and logic."

"By threatening me?"

"It's not a threat." But then he paused, obviously framing his answer, obviously knowing, as she did, that it *was* a threat. "Remove the noncompete, and I'll give you the easement. It's a mutual win."

"You call that mutual?"

He might win, but she sure wouldn't.

"I want to help you," he finally said.

"No, you don't." Of that she was certain.

"I like you, Jules."

She scoffed in disbelief.

"Last night—" he began.

"We are *not* talking about last night." She sure wasn't going to let him use her colossal lack of judgment against her.

"I knew last night. I knew about the easement last night. I couldn't…" He raked a hand through his short hair. "I couldn't let things go any further between us before I was honest."

"You want points for that?"

"I want you to know why I stopped."

Even through her anger, she had to admit it was the honorable thing to do.

But she couldn't give him credit for a single honorable thing. She wouldn't give him credit for that. He was still trying to destroy her dream by any means possible. And that was far, far below the bar anyone would set for honorable.

# Four

Caleb forced himself to keep his distance for a few days in order to let Jules think things through. Though he was anxious to hear her answer—which he had to believe would be an agreement to work together—he didn't want to press too hard. She might be stubborn, but she was smart enough to know that any other approach would be just plain foolish.

He made it to Thursday evening before he cracked. Then he sought her out, knocking unannounced on the door of her house. The lights were blazing, and he could hear a Blake Shelton tune through the open windows.

He knocked again and waited, half bracing himself, half humming with the anticipation. Despite their animosity, he'd missed her. He'd missed her a lot, and he couldn't wait to see her.

But it was Melissa who opened the door. She seemed startled to see him standing there. Her hair was in a high ponytail. She was dressed in a gauzy purple blouse and tight blue jeans. Her makeup looked fresh, and she was wearing a pair of jazzy copper earrings.

"Am I interrupting?" he asked. "Did you have a date?"

"No." She gave a quick shake of her head. "No date." But her gaze strayed to the staircase behind him.

"How's the hand?" he asked, attempting to gauge her mood.

If Jules had told her about the easement, he'd expect her to be angry. She didn't seem angry, exactly. But she did seem unsettled.

She raised her hand to show him. "Getting better fast. It really doesn't bother me much." She gave a little laugh. "The doctor said I have good aim. A quarter inch in either direction and I'd have done some real damage."

"I'm glad to hear that." Caleb realized how it sounded. "I mean, I'm glad it wasn't worse."

"Me, too." She let her hand fall to her side again.

He glanced past her into the house. "Can I speak to Jules?"

"She's not here."

The answer took him by surprise, putting the brakes on his plans.

But then he wondered if Jules was dressed up, too. Did she have a date? He hated the idea that she might.

"Can I help you with something?" Melissa asked.

The question gave him an idea.

He hadn't considered the merits of explaining the situation directly to Melissa, bypassing Jules. It was obvious to him she was the more reasonable of the two. There were even a couple of moments when he thought she would have supported some of his ideas, had it not been for Jules's staunch refusals.

Maybe he'd been talking to the wrong sister.

"You might be able to help me," he answered. "Do you have a few minutes to talk?"

She hesitated for just a second, glancing behind him again. "Sure."

He knew he should ask if it was a bad time, offer her an out if she hadn't been sincere. But it wasn't often he saw her alone. And co-opting her could turn out to be a good idea. He didn't know why he hadn't thought of it before.

She opened the door wider and moved out of his way.

Although the Parkers had been neighbors his entire life, due to the family feud he'd never been inside their house. As he moved from the small foyer, he saw that it was compact. It was mostly kitchen with aging fir cupboards and light green walls. The ceiling was off-white, and a row of three windows looked over the bay. It was a clear night, and the moon reflected off the black water.

A faded sofa and armchair took up the corner beside a stone fireplace. Nothing was new, not the brocade furniture, nor faded linoleum nor powder blue countertops. But nothing was shoddy either, and everything was clean.

"Can I offer you some iced tea?" Melissa asked, walking farther around the corner, turning down the music and moving into the kitchen.

"Thank you," Caleb answered following her.

He stopped partway, bracing his hands against one of six kitchen chairs. They were painted white, made of wood, with curved backs with dowels spaced at four-inch intervals and cotton-print cushions tied onto the seats.

She filled two glasses with ice and retrieved a pitcher of tea from the refrigerator.

He tried to guess at the refrigerator's age. It had to have been around for several decades. All he could think was that they didn't make them that sturdy anymore.

"I guess Jules didn't mention the easement," he opened.

Standing silent while she poured drinks and letting her wonder about his purpose didn't seem productive.

"She told me about it," Melissa said.

It wasn't the answer he was expecting. "She did?"

"You expect me to be hostile."

"Yes. No. On the surface, it's a setback for you."

"On the surface?" Melissa crossed to the table and handed him a glass.

She pulled out a chair, and he followed suit, sitting down cornerwise. "I would say all the way through."

She still didn't seem angry, and he had to wonder if they had a counter-strategy.

Rather than argue, he came to his point. "She didn't get back to me on it."

"She said she gave you an answer."

"In the heat of the moment, maybe. I didn't assume it was final."

"You expected her to change her mind?" Melissa's tone wasn't accusatory, more curious, and perfectly pleasant.

Again, he had to wonder if they were up to something. "I thought she'd think about it, at least consider the implications."

Melissa gave a light laugh. "I can assure you, she's fully considered the implications."

"And?" He was growing more curious by the minute.

"And she called our father. And then she called a lawyer."

"What did they say?" Caleb asked, braced and ready.

She gave a smirk. "I don't think I'll repeat what my father said."

Caleb could only imagine. "He never did like me." Caleb took a sip of the iced tea while he digested the information.

"You have a particular gift for understatement."

"Can you tell me what the lawyer said?"

"In a nutshell. That you have a case. That we also have a case. And that it'll take a long time and a lot of money to resolve it."

He rotated his glass, the ice cubes clinking against the sides. "There's no benefit in that."

"Not for you," Melissa said.

"Or for you."

She took a drink and set her glass carefully back on the wooden tabletop. "That's where you're wrong. There's a benefit to us if we win."

"You won't win."

She looked him square in the eyes. "What do you want, Caleb?"

"To be friends." He realized he meant that. "I truly don't want to annihilate the Crab Shack."

She smiled indulgently but gave an eye roll at the same time. "Forgive me if I have a hard time believing either of those things."

"I want us to work together. I meant what I said about cross-promotion."

"My father warned us about you."

Caleb had no good comeback for that, since Roland Parker had every reason to distrust the Watfords. He bought himself some time by taking another drink.

He set down his glass. "All I can say is that I'm not my father. And I get the feeling you're not your sister."

Her gaze narrowed in obvious suspicion.

He kept on talking. "I think you can see the benefits of working together. My guess is that you're very rational, and you can clearly see the downsides of a fight. It hurts us both. It'll cost a whole lot of money. And no matter who wins, we'll both be weaker and poorer for the effort."

Melissa didn't answer. She traced her fingertip down the condensation on her glass.

Caleb sat still while Blake Shelton crooned. He didn't want to make a wrong move.

She finally looked up. "You can't divide and conquer. It won't work."

He wasn't about to admit that was his strategy. "I don't want to conquer anyone. But I'm a million dollars into this project."

She seemed to think about that. "So you have a lot to lose."

"I have a lot to lose."

"Yet another reason why we shouldn't trust you."

"I understand." He did. "Tell me what I can do to—"

There was a sharp rap on the door.

Melissa jumped in her chair and her head turned sharply toward the sound.

"Expecting someone?" Caleb asked.

"No." A flush had come up on her cheeks, and her hand went to her hair. "Maybe."

The knock came again.

"You want me to get it?" he asked, seeing she was anxious.

"Melissa?" called a voice that Caleb recognized. It was Noah.

"What's *he* doing here?" Caleb had learned some

worrying things about Noah today. Things he'd planned to share with Jules and Melissa.

Melissa started to rise, but Caleb jumped up.

"There's something I need to say to him."

Before she could respond, he rounded the corner to the foyer and opened the door.

Noah was clearly taken aback by the sight of him.

"Yeah," Caleb responded to the man's unspoken question. "I'm here. What are you doing here?"

"Business," Noah said, his tone even.

"I mean what are you doing in Whiskey Bay?"

Noah's eyes became guarded.

"Been in town long?" Caleb pressed.

"It's obvious you know I haven't."

"It wasn't hard to find out."

"I wasn't hiding it."

"Caleb?" Melissa called out.

"Give me a second." Caleb had learned today that Noah was recently released from jail. "What did you do?" he asked Noah.

"About what?" Noah came back without flinching, clearly ignoring the unspoken implication.

"To get thrown in jail."

Noah paused for less than a heartbeat. "I killed a guy."

Caleb's jaw went lax.

Noah didn't elaborate.

*"On purpose?"* It was the first question that popped into Caleb's mind.

"Not really."

"And you expect me to let you anywhere near Jules and Melissa?"

"I don't think it has anything to do with you." Noah's gaze was level, his manner straightforward. He didn't seem to have the slightest inclination to cover up or apologize.

The attitude gave Caleb pause. He supposed there were a lot of ways to accidentally kill someone—from a car accident to a hunting accident to a fistfight gone bad.

Noah had gotten off with two years less a day in the county jail. And he'd been paroled for good behavior after only nine months. Upon reflection, the sentence strongly suggested mitigating circumstances.

"Are we going to have a problem?" Noah asked Caleb in an undertone.

"Was it a car accident?"

"No."

"Was there a weapon involved?"

Noah curled his fists. "No."

Seeing the unconscious gesture, Caleb was going with a fistfight gone bad.

"What did he do?" Caleb asked Noah.

A muscle twitched next to Noah's left eye. "Something unforgivable."

Caleb found he was inclined to accept the vague explanation. He had no cause to throw Noah out of the house. And that meant his time alone with Melissa was up, and he hadn't made any meaningful progress.

It was late. But Jules wasn't letting this one slide.

She pressed hard on the doorbell next to Caleb's tall cedar door. The Watford mansion was made of stone and reclaimed wood, with huge panes of glass soaring two stories high. The roof was a peak on the ocean side, and a four-car garage stretched out the back. Soft orange light shone through the windows.

Caleb opened the door.

"I can't believe you would sink that low." She didn't wait for an invitation, but marched passed him into the interior.

"How low did I sink?"

"Melissa is barely out of surgery."

"That was five days ago." He closed the door behind him.

"*That's* your excuse?"

"My excuse for *what*?"

"To badger her." Jules struggled to ignore the magnificence around her.

Caleb's house was something out of a magazine. The entry room was open and soaring. The finishing was finely polished redwood. The sconce lights gleamed as if they were plated in real gold. And she didn't dare speculate on the price of the abstract oil paintings along the stairway or the jade sculptures on the console table.

Caleb folded his arms over his chest, looking completely at home in the opulence. "That wasn't badgering. There was no badgering."

"You tried to get her to change her mind."

"No."

She couldn't believe he'd said it. "You're going to lie to me?"

"I tried to get her to change *your* mind."

His answer momentarily threw her.

He moved closer to her. "I haven't made any secret of intending to convince you we should work together."

"She's in pain." Her initial anger wearing off, Jules noticed the inlaid maple floor.

Crown molding accented a swooping ceiling, and the hallway led to a great room furnished with smooth leather and more fine wood. She didn't know what she'd expected, but it wasn't this.

"She told me she was fine," he said.

"She's not fine." Jules returned her attention to Caleb. "You took advantage of an injured woman for your own selfish desires."

"When you say it like that, it sounds creepy."

"It was creepy. Don't go to her. You want a fight? Pick me."

"I tried. You weren't home. She was. Did she talk to you about Noah?"

"Don't change the subject."

"I'm serious. Did she tell you he stopped by earlier?"

"Yes," Jules lied. This was the first she was hearing about Noah. But she didn't want Caleb to get the impression she and Melissa kept things from each other.

"You want a drink?"

"No, I don't want a drink. This is not a social call."

"Well, do you want to come in?" He gestured down the hallway to the living room. "Or would you rather stand here and fight in the foyer?"

Jules hated it, but her curiosity was piqued. She was curious about the rest of the house. She was curious about the view, and about the kitchen. His kitchen had to be so much better than hers.

She was also inappropriately curious about the rooms upstairs and, for a split second, she glanced that way.

"I can give you a tour of the house," he said.

"Not necessary."

His gestured down the hall again. "I'm guessing you have more to say?"

"I always have more to say."

He cracked a smile. "I've definitely noticed that."

"This isn't funny."

"You don't get to dictate my emotions. Shall we at least sit down?"

She agreed and started down the hall, trying hard not to be bowled over by the surroundings. It got better and better. The furnishings were gorgeous, but looked comfortable. The artistic touches were understated and classy, while the great room's high-peaked ceiling was breathtaking.

"Hi, Jules," came a man's voice.

She nearly stumbled into the sofa.

"I'm Matt," he said, rolling to his feet from an armchair. "I was with Caleb when your sister got hurt."

Jules was momentarily speechless. This man had overheard her tirade? What had she said? She scrambled to remember.

Caleb entered the room behind her. "You sure you don't want a drink? We're having beer, but I can open a bottle of wine."

She turned to glare at him, transmitting her irritation. "You have *company*?"

"Matt's a neighbor. He owns the house above the marina."

"You could have *said* something."

"It was hard to get a word in."

"Don't mind me," Matt said, a trace of laughter in his tone.

Jules turned back, embarrassed and annoyed. She wasn't here for their entertainment. "I obviously didn't know you were here."

"You didn't say anything embarrassing," Matt said. "In fact, I'm on your side. Caleb shouldn't have taken advantage of your sister in her moment of weakness."

"I didn't," Caleb protested. "And she's not in a moment of weakness. She said it herself that she was feeling fine."

"She's probably high on painkillers," Matt said. "She only thinks she feels fine."

"Shut up," Caleb said.

Jules couldn't help but appreciate Matt's support. "See? Even Matt agrees with me. It's very nice to meet you, Matt."

"Care for a beer?" Matt asked her.

"Sounds good," she said.

"Seriously?" Caleb grumbled. "To him you say yes?"

"I'm a lot more appealing than you." Matt started across the room. "Women like me."

"You've been divorced a single month, and you're already a gift to women?"

Matt held his arms wide. "What can I say?"

"He does seem very nice," Jules said in a clear tone.

"Not to mention handsome." Matt had reached a wet bar tucked in the corner of the room and bent over to open a hidden fridge.

"He is rather handsome," Jules said, content to keep the conversation two against one. "And, I bet he's not trying to undermine or destroy any of the women in his life."

Caleb's expression tightened for a second.

"She's got you there," Matt said.

"I'm not trying to destroy anyone," Caleb said.

"Glad to hear it." Jules made a show of reaching into her handbag. "If you could just sign these papers to guarantee my easement."

"Melissa said you saw a lawyer."

"I did see a lawyer."

Caleb took a couple of steps and lifted a manila envelope from a side table. "So did I. If you could just sign these papers removing the noncompete clause."

Jules paused. "Do you actually have those papers at the ready?"

He didn't respond, and she couldn't tell anything from his expression.

"Because I was bluffing," she said. She didn't have papers of any kind in her handbag.

He held up the envelope. "This is a charitable donation to the new health clinic."

She opened her bag and made a show of peering inside. "I can't even come that close. All I have are text messages on my phone."

Matt chuckled as he twisted open a bottle of beer and pushed the fridge shut with his thigh.

"You can't win," Caleb said to her.

"Neither can you."

"So, we should compromise."

"You don't want to compromise. You want me gone."

"I don't want you gone." He tossed down the envelope and moved to stand next to an armchair. "Why don't you sit down?"

Matt arrived and handed her the beer.

She glanced from one man to the other and decided she might as well sit down. If she hoped to reason with Caleb, they'd have to have a conversation. She lowered herself onto the sofa.

Caleb sat, as well.

"He's not a bad guy," Matt said.

"Sure he is. He comes from a long line of bad guys who can't stand the Parker family."

"I've got nothing against the Parker family," Caleb said.

"Then give me my easement."

"You're like a broken record."

"I only want one thing."

"I agree." Caleb lifted a half-full beer that was sitting on a coaster on the table next to him. "But it's not an easement."

"It's not?"

"What you want is for the Crab Shack to succeed."

Jules couldn't disagree with the statement, so she elaborated instead. "And for the Crab Shack to succeed, customers need to get to the parking lot."

"I'll give you the easement," he said.

"Thank you."

"As soon as you remove the noncompete clause."

"Thereby guaranteeing the annihilation of the Crab Shack. Do you think I turned stupid over the past three days?"

"I hoped you'd turned reasonable. You have no other move."

"I can fight you in court," she said.

"I can out-lawyer you a hundred times over."

"Whoa," Matt said from the sidelines.

"Care to reassess your opinion of him?" she asked Matt.

Caleb frowned at his friend.

"This is where I tap out," Matt said, finishing his beer and making to leave.

"So much for being on my side," Jules muttered.

"You should listen to him," Matt said.

"Exactly as I thought." She shouldn't be disappointed. There was absolutely no chance that Matt was going to back her against Caleb. But she'd liked Matt. She wanted him to turn out to be a good guy.

"See you later," Caleb said to Matt.

Matt gave him a nod as he exited the room.

"I guess it's just you and me," Jules said.

"Just you and me," Caleb agreed.

* * *

The door shut behind Matt.

Caleb knew it was time to change the conversation with Jules. They'd been going round and round for days now, and it had become obvious they were going to end up in court.

He hated that it would come to that. Going to court would hurt Jules the most. It would slow him down, and he'd lose money, but she'd lose everything.

She seemed to realize it, too, a dispirited expression taking over her face as she sipped the beer.

Even looking so sad, she was extraordinarily beautiful. And despite the circumstances, he liked having her in his house. She did something to it, seemed to bring it alive. He realized it was likely the last time she'd be here, and it made him feel almost as despondent as she looked.

"Did Melissa tell you what Noah said?" he asked.

If these were their final moments before the court battle began, he felt a duty to let her know about Noah's past.

"Not exactly." She hesitated. "I do know he has an idea for—" She seemed to change her mind and pressed her lips together.

"I'm not going to steal your restaurant plans, Jules."

"You want them to die on the page."

Restless, Caleb came to his feet. "It doesn't have to be this way."

"Yes it does."

"Even Melissa understands my position."

"Did she say that?" Jules asked sharply. "What did she say? What exactly happened between the two of you?"

"Nothing happened between us."

Could she be asking what Caleb thought she was asking?

"Noah showed up," he finished.

"And that stopped *what*?" She *was* asking that.

"Me trying to reason with her." He waited to see how far Jules would take her wild accusations. Caleb had no romantic interest in Melissa. He was nuts about Jules.

"Reason with her?" Jules voice went up. "Is that a euphemism for romance her?"

Before he could answer, she abandoned her beer and came to her feet.

"Is that your master plan, Caleb? Cozy up to my sister and turn her against me?"

He started to deny it, but then he stopped himself, seeing a whole new angle of attack. He guessed Jules would do almost anything to protect her sister.

"What if I am?" he asked.

"Then you're a complete and reprehensible jerk."

"I think you've already decided that."

"I'll just tell her what you're up to. That'll shut you down."

"Will it?" he asked softly. "We both know she wants to trust me." He watched the uncertainty cross Jules's face and pressed his advantage. "She wants to find a solution. She's a very beautiful woman."

"I can't believe you'd sink that low."

"I'd sink very low," he bluffed. "There's a whole lot of money at stake here."

"You stay *away* from my sister." Jules cheeks were glowing pink. Her blue eyes flashed with anger.

He held himself steady against the guilt he was feeling. This bluff was for her own good.

"If it's that important, I'll make you a deal," he said.

"I am *not* removing the noncompete."

He took a couple of steps forward, craving intimacy with her. "That's not my deal."

"What other deal is there?" She tipped her chin as he grew closer.

He wished he could take the last couple of steps, draw her into his arms and apologize for upsetting her. Of course he wasn't interested in her sister. And he'd never use Melissa's trusting nature against her. It was all Jules. Everything was Jules.

He could still taste her last kiss, and he desperately wanted another. He was acutely aware of the fact that they were alone in the house. All of their cards were now on the table and there was nothing stopping them from doing anything they wanted.

"Caleb?" she interrupted his wandering thoughts.

"Hmm?"

"The deal?"

He couldn't help a small smile. "You date me instead."

She went speechless for a moment. "That gets you where?"

He gave a shrug. "Not your concern. One date. Let me take you on one date, and I'll back off on Melissa."

Jules tilted her head to one side.

It made it even harder to keep from kissing her.

"What on earth are you up to?"

"I'm attempting to make you see things my way."

"You don't need to date me to argue with me."

"Take the deal, or leave it and I try something else."

"You try to cozy up to Melissa."

Caleb countered with an ambiguous shrug.

He'd come up with an ad hoc plan for using the date

to help Jules see reason. But if he was honest with himself, right now, he mostly just wanted the date.

"One date?" she said.

"One date."

She considered the offer, looking like she was making a very painful decision. It was hard on a guy's ego, but it was what it was.

"Okay," she finally said in a small voice and with a whole lot of uncertainty.

"Your enthusiasm is gratifying."

"We both know you're practically blackmailing me."

He gave in to the urge to move closer. "And we both know what happens when I kiss you."

She put the flat of her hand against his chest.

The warmth of it seeped through his shirt, and he couldn't stop himself from closing his eyes to savor the touch.

"Stop it," she said huskily.

"I like it when you touch me."

"I'm holding you off."

"I know."

"That's not the same as touching you."

He opened his eyes. Big mistake, because she was right there, so close.

"Do you have any idea how beautiful you are?" he asked.

"When?" she asked.

"All the time."

"When is the date?"

"Are you not feeling anything?" He didn't want to believe the physical attraction was all on his side.

She swallowed. "No."

She was lying. He'd bet the new Neo location that

she was lying. And that meant there was in fact hope. Their date could turn out to be very interesting.

"Friday night," he said.

"Fine." She dropped her hand and took a backward step.

He missed her already.

# Five

Melissa abruptly stopped sanding the old barstool with her good hand, straightening to stare across the Crab Shack at Jules. The morning sun streamed through the window behind her, highlighting the fine sawdust and making her blond hair glow like a halo.

"There's something I'm not getting," she said.

"What's not to get?" Jules sized up one of the dining tables.

"The part where Caleb asks *you* on a date."

"What's wrong with me?" Jules's plan had been to offhandedly mention tomorrow night's date with Caleb and blow past it on to more important subjects. The blowing past it wasn't working as well as she'd hoped.

"He can date anyone. I've Googled the guy and you should see some of the women who go out with him."

"Thanks, tons." Jules pretended to be offended.

Melissa waved a hand through the air. "Don't be ridiculous. That wasn't an insult. Why you?"

"That sounds like an insult." Jules pushed the table toward the center of the room, making space along the walls where Noah planned to work on the electrical system later in the day. "Were you thinking paint or stain for the barstools?"

Melissa wouldn't let it go. "There's something you're not telling me."

Her sister was too astute, but Jules had no intention of letting on that Caleb had initially targeted Melissa to romance. It would sound like Jules didn't trust her. She did.

It was Caleb she didn't trust. He was underhanded, and Melissa's instinct was to search for an amicable solution. That made her vulnerable to his bogus claims of both restaurants succeeding.

"All right," Jules said, frowning. "Maybe it's because I kissed him."

"You *what*?"

"Well, he kissed me. I suppose that's more accurate. He was the one doing the kissing. I simply…" Jules wasn't exactly sure how to finish that sentence.

Luckily, she didn't have to. Melissa jumped back in.

"Where? When? Why didn't you say something?"

"It was a nonevent. That day we were moving the pictures, while you were talking to Noah. Caleb kissed me. I kind of kissed him back. It's embarrassing, but he is pretty hot. And, well, I'm guessing he might be under the impression that I'm attracted to him. And, maybe, well, maybe he thinks if he dates me and, I don't know, sweeps me off my feet, he can change my mind about the noncompete clause. You know that's all he really wants."

Melissa stared wide-eyed through the entire explanation, which Jules realized had gone on way too long.

"You kissed him back."

"A little bit."

"Okay." Melissa rubbed the sandpaper a few strokes. "I get that you might kiss him. He's a handsome, charming guy. But why did you agree to a date? What's in it for you?" She paused. "Unless, ooh, are you genuinely interested in—"

"No!" Jules barked too quickly. "I'm not interested in him, genuinely or otherwise."

"You just admitted he was hot."

"He isn't—" Jules stopped herself. She wanted to lie as little as possible. "Okay, fine, in an objective sort of way. I'd have to be dead not to notice that Caleb is hot. And Noah's hot."

Melissa's brows went up, and she opened her mouth.

Jules bowled forward, talking louder. She wanted to get this over with. "There are a lot of hot guys in the world. That doesn't mean I'm automatically attracted to them. I have a mission when it comes to Caleb, and I'm executing part of that mission through a fake date. I think I can use it to our advantage. Period."

"Jules," Melissa said.

"What?" Jules hoped she'd put it to rest.

"He's behind you."

"Who?"

"Caleb."

Perfect. Now he had her on record admitting he was handsome. This was going to be a pain.

She felt her cheeks warm as she turned. "Hello, Caleb."

"Hello, Jules."

Silence fell.

She couldn't stand it, so she leaped in. "I was telling Melissa about our date."

"So I heard."

She walked to the next table and started to push it out of the way. "Was there something you needed?"

He immediately joined her to help move the table. "Yes. There's something I meant to tell you."

Jules realized that Melissa had to wonder why Caleb wasn't reacting to her outburst. She couldn't for the life of her come up with a reason, so she decided on the blow-past-it strategy again. Hopefully, it would work better this time.

"What was it?" she asked Caleb.

"Do you want me to leave you two alone?" Melissa asked, obviously assuming, quite reasonably, that they had things to discuss.

"You need to hear this, too," Caleb said. "What are we doing?" he asked Jules, nodding to the table now held between them.

"Stacking them all in the center of the room. Noah wants to work on the electrical today."

"Is Noah here?" Caleb asked.

"He's at the hardware store," Melissa answered.

"Good."

"Jules isn't interested in him," Melissa said.

Both Jules and Caleb turned to look at her.

"She might think he's hot, but she doesn't want to date him."

Jules realized her protestations about the date hadn't worked. Melissa thought she was genuinely attracted to Caleb.

"Don't worry about explaining," Jules told her.

"He's really not her type," Melissa said.

"It's *fine*, Melissa."

Caleb could barely hide the amusement in his tone. "Jules and I have an understanding."

"An understanding?" Melissa asked in obvious confusion.

Caleb wrapped an arm around Jules's shoulders. "She's not convinced we're a good idea, but she's agreed to give me a shot."

Jules fought not to shrug him off. Then she fought not to enjoy his touch.

"So, all that…" Melissa drew a little circle in the air. "All that song and dance about only using the date to change your mind?"

"She's in denial," he said.

"You know, I thought that had to be it," Melissa said.

Jules shot Caleb a look of frustration. He was unnecessarily complicating things.

"But I'm an optimist," he said.

She did shrug her way from his arms.

"About Noah," Caleb said, moving on. "I learned something about him that I think you two have a right to know."

"You mean his criminal record?" Melissa asked.

Jules couldn't contain her surprise. "Noah has a criminal record?"

"It's nothing serious," Melissa answered.

"What did he tell you?" Caleb asked.

"That he got into a fight."

"What happened?" Jules asked them both, trying to wrap her head around the revelation. "Was someone hurt?"

Caleb's attention was on Melissa. "You knew but you didn't tell Jules?"

"It wasn't serious," Melissa said, dusting her hands together and contemplating the barstool. "He told me about it when he applied for the contract."

Jules wasn't sure what it took to have a criminal record. "Did he assault someone? Was there a trial? Did he actually go to jail?"

"Not serious?" Caleb challenged Melissa. Then he turned to Jules. "Yes, he went to jail. The other guy died, and Noah went to jail."

Jules's stomach clenched with anxiety. "Noah is a killer?"

"It was self-defense," Melissa said staunchly. "It was self-defense, and it was an accident. I looked up the newspaper articles."

Jules didn't know how to react. She was confident Melissa had done her research, and she was sure Melissa thought Noah was harmless. But Melissa always saw the best in people. No matter how it had happened, Noah had killed someone.

Jules moved toward her sister. "You should have told me."

Melissa looked contrite. "I know. I know I should have. But, well, you know what you're like."

Jules didn't follow. "What am I like?"

Melissa's gaze flicked to Caleb. "You don't trust anyone."

"And you trust everyone. Not trusting killers is just common sense."

"He's *not* a killer," Melissa repeated. "He's a decent guy who was in a bad situation, and he deserves a second chance. Besides, his prices are half of anyone else's."

"Because he's a convicted killer," Jules felt the need to point out. "I would imagine they all charge less than their competition."

Noah's flat tone echoed across the room. "Don't worry. I'll clear out."

Jules turned, and her stomach sank. She instantly realized how judgmental her words had sounded. Seeing him in front of her, she found it impossible to believe he was dangerous. She'd been working with him for days on end, and he'd been nothing but respectful and kind.

"I'm sorry," she began.

"I'm the one who's sorry," he said. "I didn't realize Melissa had kept it to herself."

"Because it doesn't matter," Melissa said.

"It does matter," Noah said.

"You can't blame her for asking questions," Caleb said.

Noah glared at Caleb. "Who said I blamed her? I just said I'd clear out."

"We need you." Melissa rushed to Noah and grasped his arm, as if she could hold him there with her one good hand.

When Noah looked at her, his emotion was stark. It was obvious he liked Melissa. He clearly liked her very much.

"Stay," Jules said. "If it was an accident. If you were in a bad position. If it's behind you, well, Melissa is right. You deserve a second chance."

Noah seemed to hesitate.

"We do need you," Jules added. "We don't have much money, and—" She couldn't help glancing at Caleb.

His expression was taut and unreadable.

She finished her thought. "And we've run into some unexpected complications."

"Please stay," Melissa implored.

Noah stared at her as if he was mentally weighing his options. But then his expression softened and his shoulder dropped with what looked like relief. "Okay," he finally uttered.

Melissa emitted a heartfelt sigh. "Thank you."

"Thank *you*." His hand moved slowly to cover hers.

"You're sure about this?" Caleb asked Jules in an undertone.

"You're not?"

"I don't want you taking any chances."

"Funny. It seems like my biggest risk is you, not him."

Caleb didn't seem to have an answer for that, and he obviously didn't care that it was true. Jules reminded herself that it was true. He was her biggest risk because he cared only about his own interests. She had to remember that.

Jules stood in front of the mirror in the loft bedroom she was sharing with her sister.

"It seems silly not to tell me where we're going," she said to Melissa who was sprawled across the plaid bedspread on one of the two twin beds.

"I'd call it romantic, but I still think this whole date thing is strange."

Jules didn't want to rehash her decision. "Strange or not, I have to wear something."

"Go middle of the road," Melissa said, sitting up cross-legged. "That's way too fancy."

"You think?" Jules turned one way and then the other in her high heels.

The little black dress was her favorite. Held up by spaghetti straps, it was sparkly, short and sassy, with just enough swish in the skirt to make dancing fun.

"Do you want to change his mind about the easement or get him naked?"

Jules made a face at her sister. "Change his mind about the easement." But then she had to shake away an image of Caleb naked. That wasn't where she was going tonight, not at all.

"Then, unless you're heading for a high-end club… Do you think he'll take you clubbing?"

Jules couldn't begin to guess. "Last time he took me to a drive-through. Not that it was a date. I mean, there obviously wasn't a 'last time' to compare this to. But he did seem to think the drive-through would be a terrible date."

"And you jumped from that to glitz and glam?"

"You think pants? I've got skinny jeans and that leather-trimmed sweater."

"Too far the other way." Melissa unfolded her legs and came to her feet.

She headed for their shared dresser and pulled open a middle drawer.

Jules kicked off the shoes, stripped off the dress and hung it in the makeshift closet. Years ago, their grandfather had attached a piece of doweling across one corner of the room. Their grandmother had sewed a cotton floral curtain to cover it, and it had been the room's closet ever since.

"What about these?" Melissa produced a pair of snug-fitting black slacks. "Your black ankle boots with my silky pink tank. You can layer on some gold necklaces, big earrings, and you're good to go."

"You have better clothes than me," Jules couldn't help commenting as she stepped into the pants.

"I spent forever in your hand-me-downs. I deserve a few nice things."

"I think you might just have better taste." Jules didn't go out very often. That, combined with their years'-long focus on building up their savings account, meant she didn't have a particularly extensive wardrobe.

She slipped into the bright pink tank top. It was supple and soft against her skin.

"That looks great on you," Melissa said.

Jules turned to the mirror. "I think this'll work. The boots are comfortable in case we walk anywhere. But I look good from the waist up if the place is fancy."

"You look good from the waist down, too. Are you sure this is a smart idea?"

"It's the best idea I've got."

No matter how confusing the tactic might seem, Jules needed to humor Caleb to keep him away from turning his attention to Melissa.

"Your emotions are muddled," Melissa said quietly. "On some level, you want the date. Because this really isn't the best way to change his mind."

"Quit worrying, and let me try. You know he has the upper hand right now. We can bluff and bluster all we want, but we can't afford much in the way of lawyers. We have to appeal to his sense of decency."

"You think he's decent?"

"I don't know. But I'm going to find out."

Melissa put a hand on Jules's shoulder, and their gazes met in the mirror. "You're my big sister, and I respect your judgment. But you really don't have to do this."

"You're my little sister, and I respect your opinion, but I know exactly what I'm doing." Jules mustered up a carefree smile. "It's a date. It's not like I'm going bull-riding or base jumping. What's the worst that can happen?"

Melissa mimicked their father's voice. "You, young lady, could come home pregnant."

Jules couldn't help but crack a smile. "You know, I

honestly think Dad would prefer me getting pregnant to us reopening the Crab Shack."

"What if Caleb Watford was the dad?"

"Whoa," Jules intoned, letting her mind wrap itself around that. Her father hated the Watfords with a single-mindedness that had only grown over time.

"Good thing you changed out of that sexy dress." Melissa patted Jules's shoulder before letting go. "Big earrings and a chunky necklace, that's what this outfit needs."

There was a knock on the door downstairs.

"He's on time," Melissa said.

Jules felt a flutter in her stomach. It wasn't excitement, she told herself. It was anxiety.

"I'll tell him you'll be a few minutes."

As Melissa left the room, Jules focused on her jewelry box, coming up with a pair of dangling earrings with multiple gold bead drops. She found a complementary necklace, six strands with scattered gold beads of increasing size.

She made a last-minute decision to put her hair up, and swooped it into a loose topknot. She shook her head back and forth, liking the way the earrings swayed. Caleb's voice sounded downstairs, its deep timbre reverberating through her chest as she sat down on the bedside to pull on her boots.

Then she was ready. She put her hand against her stomach in an effort to quell the butterflies, took a final look in the mirror and headed for the narrow staircase.

Caleb abruptly stopped talking and watched her as she descended, a worried expression taking over his face.

"Did I get it wrong?" she asked, gesturing to the outfit. "Are we going hiking or something?"

He shook his head. "You got it right."

She relaxed a little bit. "Good. You had me worried there for a minute."

"So, where are you taking her?" Melissa asked.

"Do you really want me to spoil the surprise?"

"It's not like it's her birthday, or you're proposing or something. Why the big secret?"

"She'll see." Caleb kept his attention on Jules. "Do you want to take a jacket?"

"I don't know. Do I?"

He was wearing designer jeans, an open-collar blue striped shirt and a steel-gray blazer. Like her, he'd gone middle of the road. His outfit didn't give away a thing.

"You shouldn't be cold," he said.

She picked up her purse. "Okay, then let's do this."

"Good luck," Melissa said as they moved toward the door.

"Luck?" Caleb asked Jules.

Jules kept her tone bright, as they stepped onto the porch. "She means in trying to change your mind."

"Oh. I wasn't thinking about that at all."

"Good. It gives me an advantage."

"I was thinking about showing you a really great time."

They made it to the top of the stairs, and he opened the passenger door to his SUV.

"You can drop the act," she told him as she stepped inside.

"What act?"

"You know this isn't a real date."

"This is absolutely a real date." He shut the door behind her.

Confused by the statement, she waited until he was

settled in the driver's seat. "Listen, Caleb. I don't know what your expectations are for tonight."

He pressed the start button. "My expectations are for dinner and some interesting conversation."

She told herself to take him at his word. It seemed counterproductive to belabor the point.

"What if I'm boring?" she asked.

He backed out of the short, gravel driveway. "You couldn't be boring if you tried."

Now, there was a challenge. "Sure, I could."

"How?"

She mentally ran through a couple of ideas. "I could talk about the stock market."

"Do you know anything about the stock market?"

She didn't. "That's Melissa's area of expertise. I know. I could talk you through the process of making a turducken. It takes eight hours, and it's painstaking."

He swung the SUV onto the coastal highway. "What's a turducken?"

"A chicken inside a duck inside a turkey. It's all boneless and layered with savory stuffing. It has Cajun roots, and it's absolutely delicious."

"Sounds fascinating. Where did you go to school?"

"Oregon Culinary Institute."

"Did you like it?"

"Quit trying to make this conversation interesting. First, you have to purchase a chicken, a duck and a turkey. Personally, I like to go both fresh and organic. There's a poultry farm outside Portland that will—"

Caleb chuckled. "You're hilarious."

"You think I'm joking. I'm dead serious."

"You're going to last about five minutes."

"Hey, I could write a thesis on this stuff."

"You have to write a thesis to become a chef?" he asked.

"Papers, yes. But not a thesis. The exams involve creating and cooking dishes. I once did a spiced, seared ahi tuna that made the testers cry."

"With joy, or did you overdo the spicing?"

"I got a perfect mark. Where are we going?"

They'd turned off the main highway, taking a road that led inland.

"It's a surprise."

"We're not going into Olympia?"

"What part of the surprise concept is foreign to you?"

"I thought we'd at least be in Olympia." She looked for a road sign, trying to remember where this road led. One came into view, getting closer and closer. "The airport?" she asked. "What's on the other side of the airport?"

"Not much."

"Then where are we going?"

He gave her an odd look. "The airport."

"It's the community airport. They don't even have flights from there." She was setting aside for the moment the outlandish concept that there might be a plane ride involved in this date.

"They don't have commercial flights," he corrected.

"Are we going sightseeing?"

He smiled at that.

"We're taking a jet," he said as the airport building loomed up.

"You have a jet?" The evening was starting to feel completely surreal.

"No, I don't have a jet. Exactly how rich do you think I am?"

"Pretty darn rich from what I've seen so far."

"I don't own a private jet. I merely booked it from a service."

"Oh, well that makes a big difference," she drawled.

"It does to me. I'm not about to tie up capital in a jet I barely use."

"How very frugal of you."

He turned the vehicle into the small airport parking lot. "I like to think so."

"That was sarcasm."

"No kidding." He chose a parking spot in front of the low building and brought the SUV to a halt.

As he shut off the engine and killed the headlights, she realized she was nervous and tried to figure out why. The airport was quiet, but not deserted. She could see an agent sitting inside what looked like a plush boarding lounge. There were several planes parked beyond the chain-link fence.

But the uneasy feeling refused to leave.

Caleb came around to her side and opened the door.

She didn't move.

He held out his hand.

She turned her head. "I don't trust you."

"You don't trust me to what?"

"Am I going to end up stranded in Ecuador or Brazil?"

He looked amused. "Ecuador?"

"It occurs to me that you could dump me in some foreign country and come back and coerce Melissa."

"You have an active imagination."

"You have a conniving mind."

He crossed his arms over his chest. "Exactly how would I explain your absence?"

"You'd come up with something. Maybe you already

have a plot in the works." But as she spoke, she realized he made a good point.

Her suspicions were starting to feel silly.

"We're going to San Francisco," he said.

"That's your story." But she was joking now. She was starting to relax. "Once we're in the air, how will I know the difference?"

"You'll recognize the Golden Gate Bridge." He reached out again, offering her his hand. "When we board, the pilot can show you the flight plan."

She was willing to admit that sounded reasonable— surreal, but reasonable. "I've never flown on a private jet." She took his hand and stepped out.

"You'll like it."

"So, what's in San Francisco?"

"The original Neo restaurant."

As they crossed the nautical-themed wooden walkway that led to Neo's front entrance, Caleb tried to see the restaurant through Jules's eyes. The two-story building sat oceanfront on a peninsula that provided views of both the marina and the ocean. The salty scent of the air and gentle hum of the waves gave the restaurant its signature ambiance.

The structure was West Coast-style, as were all of the Neo locations, with soaring beams and plenty of windows. The polished wood reflected the interior light and gave a warm, welcoming glow.

They walked inside to find several other couples in the foyer. The maître d' immediately recognized Caleb, and gave him a nod of acknowledgment. But Caleb knew the maître d' would seat the customers in order. He didn't ask for preferential service. In fact, he insisted the customers were more important.

The foyer was dramatic, two full stories in height, with a river stone feature wall that camouflaged the short hallway to the restrooms. The reception desk was carved from driftwood, another feature duplicated at each of the other restaurants. The hanging lights had burnished copper shades, and occasional tables were decorated with large, earth-toned pottery vases filled with fresh flowers.

Beyond the foyer, muted saltwater fish tanks were interspersed with privacy screens that dampened sound and broke up the tables in the main dining room. Caleb planned to take Jules to the second floor where they would overlook dining tables and the open kitchen, and be parallel to one of the features—a carved redwood chandelier inset with nautical glass floats.

Jules leaned close to him, speaking beneath the murmur of conversations. "This place is stunning."

"We renovated two years ago."

"You should be taking someone else on this date."

Her words made him grin with amusement.

"You know," she elaborated. "Someone who's impressed by you, who'd be bowled over by your power and prestige, where you'd at least have a chance..."

"I got your meaning," he said.

Regular date or not, he didn't want to be with anyone but Jules right now. Their relationship was beyond complicated, but for now she was here, and that was his initial goal.

Having assisted the other customers, the maître d' approached. "Good evening, Mr. Watford."

"Hello, Fred. It's nice to see you." Caleb shook the man's hand.

"I didn't realize you were joining us tonight." Fred's gaze moved to Jules.

"It was a last-minute decision. This is Jules Parker."

"Nice to meet you, Ms. Parker. Welcome to Neo."

Jules tipped her head back to gaze at the soaring space. "This place is spectacular."

"I'm so pleased you think so," Fred responded. "Did you have a seating preference this evening?" he asked Caleb.

"Something on the second floor? On the rail?"

"Absolutely." Fred motioned to one of the hosts, who immediately came forward.

"Table seventy," Fred said.

"This way, please," the crisply dressed man offered, gesturing with his arm.

Caleb put his hand lightly on the small of Jules's back, guiding her forward.

"Be careful on the stairs, ma'am," the host cautioned over his shoulder.

The polished stair rail was subtly illuminated, and there were mini lights in the seams of the stairs, making it as safe as possible for patrons.

Caleb followed her up and waited while the host pulled out her chair and placed her napkin.

"Very nice view," she noted gazing across the room and down to the dining area below. "Is that a real ship's bell? Is everything antique?"

"It is. Most of the decor is from the twentieth century, but it's all authentic."

"I'm stealing some of these ideas."

"Good."

She turned her teasing attention to him. "You don't care?"

"It'll make it easier for us to coordinate efforts."

"You don't miss an opportunity, do you?"

"Never."

She seemed to reconsider her approach. "The Crab Shack is not going to be Neo's poor cousin."

"I never suggested that."

"Everything you've said and done is suggesting that."

"Poor cousin is a negative term."

There was a sudden rattle of dishes, and the floor beneath them vibrated.

Jules eyes widened, and she gripped the edge of the table.

"It's a small earthquake," he assured her. It wasn't the first he'd experienced in San Francisco. "This building is designed to withstand—"

But the rumbling beneath them increased. The lights swayed, and some glassware fell over, shattering. A couple of people screamed.

"Caleb?"

Caleb jumped to his feet. "Shelter under your tables!" he called to the patrons around him, projecting his voice over the rail and to the people below. "The building is earthquake-proof. Get down, but stay put. You're safer in place than trying to exit."

The shaking increased. "Everybody under the tables," he called louder. "Staff, help anyone who needs it."

He quickly moved to Jules, assisting her as she crawled under their table. "You'll be fine," he told her.

Then he looked around, seeing an older couple struggling. He quickly gave them a hand.

The shaking increased alarmingly, becoming more violent. Decorations began falling from the walls, and the dishes were cascading from their tables.

"Caleb!" Jules cried.

With a fast look around to ensure people were sheltering, Caleb rushed back to her, all but diving under his own table.

The noise grew deafening, as more items fell and people cried out in fear. He grasped Jules, pulling her close. "It'll be all right."

"I know."

"The building won't fall down."

Just then, out of the corner of his eye, he saw the redwood chandelier shift. One of the anchor bolts popped and the whole contraption dangled precariously, the glass floats raining down. "Look out!" he cried.

Then the chandelier crashed two stories to the floor.

Caleb craned his neck, immensely relieved to see it had hit the open kitchen instead of a table.

"Anybody hurt?" he called down.

"I don't think so." It was Fred's voice, and Caleb saw that a group of staff members had clustered with him around the rock wall. That was a good decision. The wall was anchored in concrete set deep in the earth.

As the shaking started to subside, Caleb could see flames licking up from the gas grill, through the redwood chandelier.

He clasped Jules's hand and looked her straight in the eyes. "Everybody needs to get out of here."

"What can I do?"

"Help that older couple." He pointed. "I have to make sure the gas is turned off."

She nodded.

"You okay?" he asked.

"I'm fine." She looked calm and capable.

He was grateful for that.

The shaking had all but stopped, and he stood again. The lights flickered but stayed on.

"There are five exits," he called out. "One in each

corner on the first floor, plus the main entrance where you all came in. There's no need to panic, no need to run, but you should leave the building and gather at the back, away from the beach. Staff will help anyone who needs it. I repeat, slowly leave the building and gather at the back away from the beach."

He leaned down to Jules who was crawling out from under the table. "You're good?"

"I'm good. Go. Put out the fire."

Caleb left her to help the older couple and made his way downstairs. Fred was there to meet him, along with the manager and the head chef.

"The gas needs to be shut off," he said.

"We're working on the back kitchen connections," said Kiefer, the head chef. "But I'm worried there might be leaks in the lines."

A couple of staff members arrived with fire extinguishers and doused the flames in the central kitchen.

"Is there a main valve outside?" Caleb asked.

"Behind the kitchen, but you need a wrench," one of the staff replied.

"Where can I find a wrench?"

Fred answered, "There should be one in the basement, on the bench in the utility area."

"Make sure everyone evacuates," Caleb told Fred.

"Yes, sir."

Then Caleb spoke to the manager, Violet. "You've called the fire department?"

"The lines are jammed, but we'll keep trying."

"Shut off everything you can," he directed Kiefer. "Absolutely no open flames."

The lights went off, sending up a collective gasp from the people who were still shuffling their way out the doors. The battery lights came on immediately. It was dim, but people would be able to find their way.

"We have to assume we're on our own for a while," Caleb said. He could only imagine emergency resources were stretched thin. And there could be damage to roadways. "Who knows first aid?"

"Three of the kitchen staff are certified," Violet said, "along with me."

"Grab whatever we have for first aid kits, and check out as many people as you can. Get someone to distribute bottles of water." Caleb caught a small movement and saw that it was Jules.

"What can I do?" she asked.

"I need to find a wrench in the basement."

"I'll help."

His first instinct was to say no, to tell her to go outside to safety, but he wanted to keep her with him. He told himself a second set of eyes would help find the tools quickly. And the priority was to shut off the main gas valve.

"This way," he said, wending his way through the upturned tables toward the basement stairs. "There's glass all over the floor," he warned her.

"I'm wearing boots."

"Good choice."

"We have Melissa to thank for that."

Caleb opened the basement door. He thought he caught another whiff of gas, and he knew they had no time to waste.

# Six

Three hours later, with the gas shut off and the customers safely on their way home, a firefighter approached Jules and Caleb at the front of the building.

"Are you okay, ma'am?" he asked her.

She was tired and a little cold, but otherwise she was fine.

"I'm good," she told the man in the heavy jacket and helmet.

He turned his attention to Caleb, removing his glove to offer a handshake. "Zeke Rollins, Station 55."

Caleb shook the man's hand. "Thanks for your help."

"You'll need the building cleared by an engineer before anybody goes inside or you start repairs."

"Already set up for tomorrow," Caleb replied. "Except for the smashed grill area, we're hopeful it's superficial."

"I hope you're right. You're definitely at the epicenter of the damage. We lost a couple of historic buildings down the block. Luckily they were empty."

"Anyone seriously hurt?" Jules asked. She'd been immensely relieved to learn the customers at Neo had gotten away with minor cuts and bruises.

"A few broken bones, and one patient is in surgery. But it could have been a lot worse."

Jules nodded her agreement. She'd never been in an earthquake before. It had been terrifying.

"We're hearing it was a 6.0," Zeke said. "Good thing it was offshore. You won't reenter the building tonight?"

"We won't," Caleb said. "I've got security posted on the doors. I'm meeting the engineering firm in the morning, and we'll take it from there."

"Glad to hear it. And I'm glad you're both all right."

"Thanks, again," Caleb said.

Zeke gave him a clap on the shoulder before taking his leave.

"You were really great in all this," Jules felt compelled to tell Caleb.

He'd taken charge, made sure people didn't get hurt, ensured the building didn't burn down.

He gave a shrug. He'd long since discarded his blazer, and the sleeves of his shirt were rolled up. He had a scrape on one cheek, and there was dirt on his arms. He looked confident, capable and strong, if a little tired around the eyes.

"What now?" she asked him, following his gaze to the building. It looked perfectly normal from outside, but she knew the interior was a mess.

"You must be hungry," he said.

She hadn't really thought about it. "I meant for Neo."

"We'll do the repairs." He didn't sound particularly worried.

"Just like that?"

"We have good insurance. We'll have to close for a few days, but I'm confident we'll be back in business soon."

"You are an optimist." She found herself admiring his attitude.

"Let's go." He surprised her by looping an arm around her waist. Then she surprised herself by leaning in.

"Where?"

"Somewhere they'll feed us. Do you mind heading home tomorrow instead of tonight?"

"No problem."

Transportation home seemed like the least of their worries. She'd have to call Melissa. Then it occurred to her that Melissa didn't even know she was in San Francisco. Wow. That was going to be an interesting phone call.

"I'm sure you'll want a shower," Caleb said as they made their way toward the parking lot.

She frowned as she looked down at her dirt-stained clothes. She'd torn a hole in the knee of her pants. "These are Melissa's."

"Clothes can be replaced."

"I know. I didn't mean that the way it sounded. I was just thinking that she doesn't even know I left Olympia."

"I didn't mean to sound critical."

"You didn't. Buying new clothes is nothing. I guess I'm a little rattled."

He gave her a squeeze around the waist. "We're all a little rattled. You were fantastic back there. Why don't you call Melissa while we drive?"

They'd picked up a rental car at the San Francisco airport, and he unlocked the doors.

Jules realized she didn't have her phone. It was the first time she'd even thought of it. "I left my purse inside the restaurant. My phone, my keys, my credit cards."

Caleb slid his phone from the pocket of his pants and held it out to her. "My wallet is in my pants. But I haven't a clue where I left my jacket." He paused, leaning on the door as she got in. "This didn't go exactly the way I'd planned."

She knew she shouldn't smile, but she did. She accepted his phone. "I don't think tonight went the way anybody planned."

"It seemed like such a good idea."

"I did like your restaurant," she admitted. "Though I guess it'll look different after tonight."

"We'll make it better." He pushed the door shut.

When he entered on the other side, she handed back his phone. "Password."

He punched it in. But before handing the phone back to her, he scrolled through some messages.

"Matt's worried," he said out loud. "He knew we were coming down here."

"Do you need to call him?"

Caleb typed in a couple of words. "It can wait." He handed her back the phone.

She dialed while he navigated their way from the near-empty parking lot.

It took Melissa a couple of rings to answer.

"Did I wake you?" Jules asked.

"Not really. Why? What's going on? Did you lose your phone?"

"I'm using Caleb's."

*"Really?"* There was clear speculation in her voice.

"It's nothing like that." Jules couldn't help glancing at Caleb.

He seemed focused on driving.

"We're in San Francisco," she said.

"What are you doing in San Francisco? Wait a minute. They had an earthquake in San Francisco."

"I know. I felt it."

"What happened? Are you okay?"

"I am. The Neo restaurant was pretty badly damaged." Jules gave her sister an abbreviated version of the evening, assuring Melissa that she was unharmed and that they were staying the night.

"I guess that explains it," Melissa said.

"Explains what?" Jules couldn't imagine what tonight's event could possibly explain.

"Dad called. He was trying to get hold of you and wanted to know where you were."

Again, Jules glanced over at Caleb. "You didn't tell him who I was with, did you?"

This time Caleb looked back.

"Of course I didn't," Melissa said. "It's my hand that's injured, not my brain."

"Thank goodness."

Caleb smirked. "You are hard on a man's ego, you know that?"

"Your ego's just fine."

"What?" Melissa asked.

"Nothing. Don't tell him."

"I won't tell him. Why would I tell him? You get some sleep. I'll see you tomorrow."

"I will," Jules said. "Thanks."

Jules ended the call, looking up to see they were pulling into Blue Earth Waterfront Hotel.

"You don't think this is overkill?" she asked him. "All I need is a burger and some hot water."

"Their beds are very comfortable," Caleb said as he

brought the car to a halt at the valet. "And they'll have twenty-four-hour everything. It's nearly midnight, and I don't want to take a chance."

"A chance on your every whim not being satisfied?"

"On having to eat a cardboard something from a vending machine."

The valet appeared and Caleb unrolled his window. "Checking in?" the valet asked.

"We'd like two rooms."

"Certainly, sir." The man stood back, keyed his mic and asked about availability as he turned away.

He was back in a moment. "We can offer you two superior view rooms on the thirty-second floor, with upgraded soaker tubs and king-size beds."

"That'll be fine," Caleb said, releasing his seat belt.

Jules followed suit, deciding she was through arguing. An upgraded soaker tub sounded like a slice of heaven.

A waiter set up the room service order at a table in the corner of Caleb's hotel room. The man added a rose in a narrow crystal vase and lit two candles on the white tablecloth, making the setup very romantic.

After he left, Caleb blew out the candles and set them aside along with the rose.

He considered the table for a moment then decided it looked naked, and he put everything back. He relit the candles and dimmed the overhead lights.

He was about to knock on the connecting door, when he changed his mind. Cursing himself for his indecision, he strode across the room, blew out the candles and removed the romantic touches.

Then he went back to the connecting door and gave a knock.

Jules opened it from the other side. She'd showered and changed into the exercise pants and T-shirt the hotel had sent up. Caleb was dressed in a similar outfit.

She leaned on the half-opened door, her half-dried hair wispy around her freshly scrubbed face. "You did this on purpose, didn't you?"

"Connecting rooms?"

She nodded, arranging her expression in comical suspicion.

"You heard the entire conversation."

The connecting rooms were happenstance. Though Caleb supposed the valet could have taken one look at Jules and decided to do Caleb a big favor. He thought back to the man's nametag. It was Perry something. He should give Perry a big tip.

Not that he had any expectations. He was more than certain that dinner would be the end of their date. Still, Perry's effort was appreciated.

"Well, they're really great rooms," she said, saunter-ing into his room.

"I'm glad you like them."

"What did you order?"

"You said you wanted burgers."

"You ordered burgers at a five-star hotel?"

"I did."

She turned to face him and put on a mock pout. "That's all you *ever* buy for me."

"You want me to send them back?"

She pulled out one of the chairs. "I know you know I'm joking."

He joined her, taking the other chair. "You're in a very relaxed mood."

"I'm too tired to do anything else."

"I got us wine instead of milk shakes."

"Good call." She lifted the silver warmer from her plate. It took her a second to react. "That's not a hamburger."

"Did they get the order wrong?"

"You're such a comedian."

He removed his own warmer. "Lobster chanterelle agnolotti. I hope that's okay."

She leaned in. "It smells fantastic."

"Chardonnay?" He lifted the bottle.

"Yes, please."

He poured. "I think I should get a do-over."

She watched the golden liquid cascade into the crystal glass. "A do-over of this dinner? So far it seems pretty great."

"A do-over of the date. I take back what I said to you about the drive-through that night. Nearly being killed in an earthquake is the worst date ever."

"We survived," she noted, raising her glass.

He touched his to hers. "I still want to try again."

"Why?"

"What do you mean why? Because everything that could possibly go wrong did. Look at us." He gestured to their workout clothes, bare feet and damp hair.

"I think I look terrific."

He agreed.

"And I'm seriously comfortable." She took a bite of the agnolotti and chewed. "Oh, man. This is delicious. You don't need a do-over, Caleb."

He knew what she meant was that she didn't want another date. He shouldn't be disappointed. He had no right to be disappointed. She only agreed to this date under duress.

He wasn't even sure what he'd hoped to achieve. Whatever it was, he hadn't come close to achieving it.

At least he'd kept her alive. He had that going for him.

He gave up and began eating.

"It's funny," she said between bites. "Years ago, when I had that crush on you, and when I was a typical rebellious teenager, I spun a silly fantasy about thumbing my nose at my father and riding off into the sunset with you."

"Tell me more." Caleb would ride off into the sunset with her any old time she wanted.

She didn't react to his question. "But when it happened for real, all I could do was hope my father never found out. I can't even imagine how he'd react to this."

"Will you tell him?"

"I'm never going to tell him."

"You keep a lot of secrets from your father?"

"Don't you?"

"My life doesn't have much to do with my father anymore." Caleb's parents had moved to Arizona years ago.

Jules had stopped eating and was watching him more closely. "When you were younger?"

"Kedrick and I didn't always see eye to eye." That was an understatement. There wasn't much about his father he admired.

"My dad hated sending Melissa and me to Whiskey Bay. He wanted to leave the bad memories behind. But we loved going, and our grandparents loved having us there."

"I know your dad fought with mine."

"There was bad blood between them from the day they were born."

"So you know about our grandfathers' feud."

"I know the basics," she said. "Your grandfather stole the woman my grandfather loved."

"Then your father stole my father's girlfriend," Caleb returned. "That should have made things even."

"Except that your father bullied my father his entire childhood, then had him arrested the minute he fought back."

"I don't think that's quite the way it went."

Kedrick had told Caleb the story years ago.

"That's exactly the way it went," she said.

"It's always a risk going after another guy's girlfriend," he countered.

"Are you saying my father was at fault?"

He shook his head. "I'm saying your father threw the first punch. No, that's not what I'm saying. I'm just sharing information. I'm telling you the story the way I heard it. Your father knocked out my father's front teeth."

"He was strongly provoked."

"Okay." Caleb was more than sorry they'd gotten into this argument. "Let's leave it at that."

"And he was arrested," she continued.

"He only ended up with probation." It was on the tip of Caleb's tongue to remind her that his own father had required dental surgery.

But he stopped himself. He didn't know who had said what, and how the incident had escalated, but it seemed like both of the teenage boys had lost out.

"By the time the case was settled, it was too late." Jules's voice rose with emotion. "My dad had lost his scholarship. While your family could afford Stanford or any other college your father wanted, because your grandfather had, years earlier, swindled my grandfather and stole the woman he loved."

Caleb was through defending his father, especially

because there was every chance Jules's version of the story was true. But his grandfather was another story.

"She freely chose Bert over Felix." Of that, Caleb was certain.

"Yeah, well I'm not so sure she was a prize."

"That is my grandmother you're talking about." It didn't take a genius to feel the conversation going way off the rails, but Caleb felt honor-bound to defend his grandmother, Nadine.

"Your grandmother agreed to marry the first who made his fortune." The disdain in Jules's tone was clear.

"Maybe she couldn't decide between them," he offered.

"A woman can always decide."

"You're an expert?"

"I'm a woman."

"Yes, you are definitely that."

She took a swallow of her wine. "I'm saying, if she let money make the choice for her, then she wasn't in love with either of them."

"Maybe she was in love with both of them."

"That's not possible. You can love two men, but you can't be *in love* with two men."

"I saw my grandparents together. They seemed very happy."

Jules's smile was cynical. "I'm sure they were very comfortable together what with the mansion and the Rolls-Royce they bought after your grandfather swindled my grandfather."

"I'm sure that's the way you heard it."

"That's the way it happened."

Caleb knew it had been emotionally complicated, but the business deal was straightforward. "Your grandfather bought my grandfather's half of the Crab Shack."

"For twice what it was worth."

"They had it appraised."

"They'd made a gentleman's agreement a year before the appraisal, when the property value was lower, after your grandfather stopped putting in any effort to build the business."

Caleb took a drink of the wine. It was crisp and tart. A shot of alcohol was exactly what he needed right now. It was easy to see how the difference in perspective had caused so much bad blood. But he didn't want to fight about it.

"We're not all bad guys, Jules." He hated that her low opinion of his family included him.

"The facts seem to show otherwise."

"How can I change your mind?"

"Easiest thing in the world for you to do." She let the statement hang.

She didn't have to finish it. If he capitulated, she'd believe he was a nice guy.

"You saw Neo," he said instead. "You saw what I can do, what I can build. I can help you with the Crab Shack."

"But you won't, Caleb. You won't help me. You'll only help you. Of all the chances I might take in this life, trusting a Watford is *not* one of them."

"I know my father's not a nice guy, but I've never done anything to hurt you."

She gave a sad smile and set her napkin on the table, rising. "I should go."

"Don't." The last thing in the world he wanted her to do was go.

"I'm not sure what you expected out of this, Caleb. But this date thing is not going to work. No amount of fine food and fancy wine is going to change my mind."

Caleb rose with her. "I wish we could go back."

"Back to what? When were we ever in a good place?"

He closed in. "Back to the part where you wanted to run away with me."

Her expression turned calculating. "Are you saying you'd walk away from Neo?"

He laughed softly at himself. "You're too quick for me, Juliet Parker. I can't even hope to keep up."

"You know that's not true."

"It's entirely true."

She pushed back her damp hair. "The truth is, you're more cunning than I could ever hope to be."

"I'm not cunning." He completely lost his edge around her.

Her tone softened on a sigh. "You're dangerous, Caleb."

"The last thing I want to do is hurt you."

She started to say something, but seemed to stop herself.

He touched his index finger to the bottom of her chin, tipping her head ever so slightly. "Can this date at least end with a kiss?"

"Caleb." She sounded sad.

"I really want to kiss you, Jules."

The silence stretched.

Her blue eyes blinked once. "You know what's going to happen if you kiss me."

"I'm going to want you so bad it might kill me?"

The defensiveness slipped away from her expression. "We step over that line, we can't control ourselves."

He didn't have a counter to that. He knew she was right. Still, he didn't care. This was too powerful to let slip away. "And what does that tell you?"

Her shoulders relaxed an inch. "We have chemistry."

"We have chemistry. That's not a crime. It's not going

to hurt anybody. It's just you and me, Jules, maybe for the one and only time."

The silence stretched again.

"If we do this," she said.

Anticipation nearly burst through his chest.

"What happens in this hotel room has to stay in this hotel room. We can't talk about it. We can't think about it. We can't ever, *ever* do anything like this again."

He didn't hesitate. "Deal."

Her head tilted to the side. "Did we just agree on something?"

"We did."

"You don't have a counter, a caveat, a condition?"

"None."

She moved her hand, and their fingertips brushed together. A small smile curved her lips. "Then what are you waiting for?"

He stopped waiting.

Caleb's kiss nearly buckled Jules's knees. A rational part of her brain told her this was a bad idea. But there was a more powerful part loving the feel of Caleb's strong arms around her. She leaned into his body, leaned into his kiss, let the fear and uncertainty of the night, of their circumstances, of her world slip completely away.

She pressed her palms on his arms, sliding them up over his muscled shoulders, along his back until she'd wrapped herself around him. She opened to his kiss, tasting the sharp wine, inhaling his musky scent, feeling the power of his heartbeat thud right through her skin.

His kisses grew deeper. His hands slipped down her back, finding the seam between her pants and her T-shirt. When his fingertips feathered along her skin, she shivered. He wrapped his hands around her shirt, drew back and slowly peeled it over her head.

Coming out of the shower, she hadn't bothered with her bra, so her breasts were bare to his gaze.

"Beautiful," he whispered under his breath.

She pulled off his T-shirt, smiling as she gazed at his broad chest, his perfect pecs, the strength in his arms and shoulders.

"Beautiful," she told him in return.

He smiled at that. "I like the way we're agreeing on things."

She trailed her fingers along his washboard stomach. "It's better when we get along."

"Much better."

"Let's see what else we can agree on."

"We're overdressed," he said.

She found herself grinning. She playfully hooked her thumbs under the waistband of her pants.

He did the same, and they both stripped off the last of their clothes.

"Better," he said, his gaze feasting on her.

"Better," she agreed, doing a visual tour of his magnificence.

"You're too far away," he said, taking her hand and drawing her to him.

"I can agree to that."

"You're talking too much."

"I don't think that's a—"

His lips descended on hers again.

Okay, she'd give him that one. The kiss bloomed between them, and she sank deeper into his embrace. His skin was hot against hers. She reveled in the feel of his contours, the dips and hollows, the bulges fitting so neatly against her own.

"You're so soft," he muttered.

"You're so hard."

He coughed out a surprised laugh.

"I didn't mean it that way." She paused, desire ramping up inside her at the feel of him. "Okay, maybe I did."

"We're still agreeing," he said. "I am hard, very hard, and I want you very much."

"I want you, too." She drew back to look into his eyes. "Very much."

He kissed her forehead, the tip of her nose, her cheek, then her temple, then he moved his way down her neck. "You smell amazing. You taste amazing."

She let her hands roam freely, covering him from his shoulders to his thighs, touching everything in between, while her heart rate sped up, her breathing accelerated and her skin heated in the breeze from an open window.

The traffic below was a steady hum. Caleb's breathing rushed past her ear. His phone pinged, but they both ignored it. The outside world meant nothing right now.

He took her hand, led her the few steps to the bed and swept back the covers.

She sat down on the crisp sheet, and he gently eased her back.

"Oh, this is going to be good," she said.

"I so agree."

His hot, heavy body covered hers. His hand closed over her breast, and the most intense, exquisite sensation zipped from her nipple to her abdomen.

She gasped.

"Good?" he asked, and he did it again before waiting for her answer.

She gave a small moan, and her hand clenched his shoulder, holding on to him as an anchor while the world began to spin around her.

Her hips arched, and she pulled him to her, watching his expression as their intimacy increased.

"Oh, Jules." His gray eyes darkened to pewter, and his free hand moved to the small of her back, tipping her to him.

Her entire world shifted to the touch of his body. He was hard and hot, and tantalizingly close. Nothing mattered. Nothing existed. Her primal brain clamored for the release he could bring.

She flexed, and he groaned, and their bodies melded together in perfect unison. He didn't pause in his motion, sliding in and out, gaining speed, then slowing down, then speeding up again.

She clung tight, letting him take her higher. Her legs wrapped around him. Her mouth sought his. And when they finally had to breathe, she kissed his neck, licking, tasting, drinking in the complex flavors that were Caleb.

Her hands gripped his back. He covered her breast. He kissed her mouth, probing deeply with his tongue while his thrusts grew harder and faster.

She felt herself float, go disembodied, beyond controlling her actions and reactions. She let it go, curled against him, felt the rush of desire hit a crescendo. Then she cried out his name, and his body stiffened. His guttural rasp echoed in the room as convulsions of pleasure overtook them both.

It took long minutes for Jules to spiral down. Caleb's weight felt good. The warmth of his body was comforting. His breathing was raspy. She liked it. She also liked the solid beat of his heart that seemed to sync with her own.

"Should I move?" he asked, twirling his fingers through her hair.

"Not yet."

There was a smile in his voice. "I have to say, we're batting a thousand here."

"Maybe we should hold really still and stay quiet."

He chuckled. "Before we can mess anything up?"

"That's what I was thinking."

"There's absolutely nothing I want to fight with you about."

"Good."

He cradled her face and gave her a tender kiss.

She couldn't help but think that this was perfect. They were perfect in this moment, and all was right with the world.

"Can we just stay here forever?" she asked.

"It's worth a shot."

Holding Jules in his arms, Caleb had lain awake for a long time. For a while, he'd actually hoped she'd have a change of heart, and this could be the start of something between them.

But eventually, he'd fallen asleep, and in the morning she was gone. The door between the two rooms was closed tight.

On the drive back to Neo, he'd tried to broach the subject of their night together, but she'd cut him off, citing the terms of their deal. It was obvious, even now, three hours later, that she intended to stick to her guns.

He'd managed to retrieve her purse and cell phone. That, at least, earned him a smile.

She scrolled through her messages. "Six calls from my dad."

She pressed a button and put the phone to her ear.

Caleb knew he should walk away and give her some privacy. But his curiosity won out. While the engineers combed through the building, and the electricians and gas fitters readied their gear to get to work, he stayed put.

"Hi, Dad," she opened.

There was a pause.

"She did? She didn't need to call you." Jules glanced Caleb's way. "Everything turned out fine."

Caleb could easily guess the other side of that conversation.

"On business. I came here on business."

The voice on the other end was indistinct, and Caleb couldn't hear any words, but the tone was obviously impatient. Part of him wanted to take the phone and tell Roland Parker to back off already. Roland might be bitter about his upbringing and want to forget all about Whiskey Bay, but Jules didn't. She hadn't done anything wrong. She was an adult, and she didn't have to explain herself to him.

"Checking out the competition." She looked at Caleb again, her expression appearing decidedly guilty this time.

"It doesn't matter. The important thing is I'm fine."

She paused again.

"I am. There was some damage to a few businesses, but it's all repairable."

Caleb's gaze moved to the front of Neo. He sure hoped it was repairable. Although he supposed anything was repairable. It only depended on time and money.

"I'm going home today," she said.

Roland started talking again, or maybe it was shouting from the expression on Jules's face.

"Did she tell you that? Then she is. No, we're not coming home."

Jules pressed her lips tightly together as she listened. "Dad. Dad, stop. It's *our* money."

Caleb was itching to grab the phone again.

"We've been through all that." Jules turned her back on Caleb, but she didn't walk away. "We both know how you feel about it, but nothing has changed. We're doing this. Goodbye, Dad."

A pause.

"Yes."

Another pause.

"No."

She turned back, shaking her head and gritting her teeth.

"Maybe soon. Goodbye." She ended the call.

"Everything okay?" Caleb asked.

"It's fine."

"It didn't sound fine."

"That's just the way he is. Sometimes he frets. He's convinced I was hurt worse in the earthquake than Melissa admitted, and that I'm glossing over it."

"You want to send him a quick photo to show you're healthy?"

"Of me in front of Neo? Yeah, that'll throw gasoline on the fire."

"You should stop in and see him."

"When?"

"Now."

She frowned. "He's in Portland, Caleb."

"You're about to fly home."

"That's Olympia. I don't have a spare day to drive down to Portland. Are you trying to delay construction at the Crab Shack even more? Is that what last night was about?"

He gave her a hard look. "Last night had nothing to do with the Crab Shack or Neo or anything else related to business. And I sure didn't plan the earthquake. Hell, if I could do that, I wouldn't need Neo or anything else to make money."

She had the grace to look embarrassed. "Sorry."

He moved closer. "Don't be sorry. Last night was complicated."

"Which is why we agreed not to talk about it. I was wrong to bring it up."

"But now that you have…" He fought an urge to reach for her hands. He wanted to touch her. He felt like he had a right to touch her.

"No," she said sharply. "I didn't. I shouldn't. I won't do it again."

He regrouped, knowing this wasn't the time or place. "Obviously, I'm going to be here awhile, maybe a couple of days. You can take a cab to the airport and get the plane. I'll tell them to expect you. The jet will stop in Portland, and you can see your dad for an hour."

Her expression was incredulous. "The jet will stop in Portland?"

"It's on the way."

"So, what, we'll just pop down and land."

He fought a smile. "That's exactly how it works."

"And how do I explain it to my father?"

"Tell him you had a stopover. You don't have to go into detail." He fought an urge to ruffle her hair. "You know, you'd be the worst covert operative ever."

"And you'd be the best. That's one of the things that scares me about you. I can never tell what you're up to."

He softened his tone. "I like it that way."

"Don't." She meant don't get intimate.

"I won't. I'm sorry. I'll call you a cab. You don't have to wait around here any longer."

Much as he hated for her to go, she had to get back. And he had to get started assessing the damage.

# Seven

Jules had practiced her lie over and over on the short taxi ride from the Portland airport to her father's town house. He was obviously baffled when he opened the door to find her on the porch.

"I had a stopover," she said, taking Caleb's advice and keeping the explanation short. "I thought I'd come by and say hi."

"What's wrong?"

"Nothing's wrong."

"You sounded funny on the phone."

"It was an unsettling night." She silently acknowledged to herself that it had been unsettling in far more ways than one. "Can I come in?"

"What kind of question is that?" He frowned as he stepped out of the way.

She realized it had been too much to expect that he'd be in a good mood. "I have an hour or so, and I thought we could talk."

"About what?"

"I've got some pictures of the construction." She opened her purse to retrieve her phone.

He waved her away as he closed the door behind them. "I don't want to see them."

"We've got a carpenter helping us. He's really good, and his prices are reasonable."

"You should come home. You should both come home, find real jobs, give up that run-down, ramshackle restaurant. There are a lot of nice men in Portland."

Jules mind went involuntarily to Caleb, and she quickly banished the picture.

"You know we want to do this, Dad. We think we can make it work, and we promised Grandpa."

"You should never have made that promise to your grandfather. And he should never have asked you. I should contest the will."

"You're not going to contest the will."

Although her father would have loved nothing better than to sell the land under the Crab Shack as well as her grandfather's house, no court in the country would overturn the will, and he knew it.

"You're going to lose all your money."

Jules took a seat in the compact living room. "We told you, we're willing to take that chance."

"You dragged your little sister along on this misadventure."

Jules clenched her purse on her lap. "Melissa is perfectly capable of making up her own mind."

"She follows you. She always has."

"But she argues with me when she doesn't agree."

Roland scoffed. "Don't give me that. You know you're the one in charge."

"I'm not—" Jules stopped herself, realizing the futility of going around and around on the issue.

"I wanted you to know I was fine, that we're doing fine. I thought you might be worried."

"When I think of the two of you next door to *that family*," he spat.

"It's only Caleb now. Kedrick moved to Arizona."

Her father pounced. "How do you know that?"

She realized she'd made a mistake. "It's a small neighborhood."

Roland's eyes narrowed. "That's a lot of detail."

"It's not."

"How did you hear so much about that family?"

"We've run into Caleb and a few of the other neighbors." She tried to move the conversation past the Watfords. "Matt Emerson owns the marina now and lives in the house above. It's really grown. And TJ Bauer bought the O'Hara's place and rebuilt. Ours is the only original house left."

"The land is worth a fortune by now. Selling is the only logical choice."

Something in his tone gave Jules pause.

"Do you need money?" She hadn't thought of it from that angle before.

Her father had never made a lot as a hardware store manager. They'd never talked much about money, in general. She and her sister had grown up in a very modest household without any extras.

He glared at her. "I can take care of myself."

"It was your family home."

Her grandfather might have willed it to Jules and Melissa, but her father had an equal moral call on the money tied up in the property—which was the only family legacy the Parkers had.

"This is about you and your foolish idea, and my father's irresponsible decision to have his pipe dream cross generations. As your father, it's my responsibility to save you from yourself."

Jules felt her spine stiffen. She loved her father, but he was irrational when it came to Whiskey Bay, and he was just plain wrong on this. It was a dream worth pursuing.

She realized she shouldn't have come here. She'd thought she might be able to make it a bit better. But she was only making it worse. She made a show of looking at her watch, and she came to her feet.

"As an adult, it's my responsibility to make my own decisions."

"You don't know these people."

She knew them better than he could ever imagine. She didn't trust Caleb, but she did know him, intimately. Last night tried to rush back into her brain, but she fought it off.

"I know me, and I know Melissa, and I know what Grandpa wanted. I'm doing the right thing, Dad. I hope you'll see that someday."

"I hope I'm not around long enough to see you ruined."

"Can you at least have a little faith?"

He didn't answer.

She gave a sad smile, crossed to his chair and bent down for a quick hug. "I hope you're around for a long, long time."

He gave a grunt.

She left the town house and headed for the corner where she could hail a cab. Her father's harsh words fought with an image of Caleb.

Last night might turn out to be one of her biggest

regrets in life, but it was also one of her most fantastic experiences. And right now it was a balm to everything else.

She stopped fighting and let the memories of Caleb crowd in.

Caleb had spent nearly a week in San Francisco. Jules invaded his thoughts at every turn, while he ensured the building was safe and the repairs got underway. His marketing staff was busy planning an exciting reopening event, and the community support had been enormous. As soon as things were under control, he left the manager in charge and flew back to Whiskey Bay.

Back home, his first interest was definitely Jules, so he made his way down to the Crab Shack.

Coming up on the building, he couldn't believe what he was seeing.

It was Jules. She was on the roof. Noah was up there with her, tools hanging from his belt as he set up the first row of cedar shingles.

"Hi, Caleb," Melissa greeted him, coming out onto the patio.

Noah turned and looked down.

"That's not happening," Caleb said to Noah, nodding his head in Jules direction.

"She's not using the nail gun," Melissa said.

"She's coming down *right now*," Caleb said in a booming voice that caught Jules's attention.

"It's not hard," she told him, walking down a plank on the steep pitch toward the edge of the roof.

"Stay back from the edge," he warned her.

She seemed completely unconcerned. "I'm not going to fall off the roof."

"Get her down from there," he told Noah.

"I work for her," Noah said.

"Noah wanted to hire an assistant to do the roof," Melissa said to Caleb.

"We don't need to pay for an assistant," Jules said.

"This is ridiculous." Caleb marched to the ladder and began climbing.

"Go away," Jules told him. "This is none of your concern."

He wanted to argue that it was most definitely his concern. Since last weekend, everything about her felt like it was his concern. He wasn't about to stand back and watch her get hurt or worse.

"Come down, Jules."

Her expression turned mulish as she crossed her arms over her chest. She looked adorable in dusty blue jeans, a red plaid shirt and leather work boots. Her braid stuck out of a red baseball cap, and she had a measuring tape clipped onto her waistband.

He wanted to take a picture. More than that, he wanted to throw her over his shoulder and carry her like a fireman down the ladder. Then maybe he'd keep going, all the way to his house, all the way to his bed, where he'd strip off those work clothes and join her in his tile shower.

He stepped onto the roof. "I'll be the assistant."

He didn't have a ton of time to spare, but there was no way he was risking her.

"We don't want your help," she said. "And we don't trust your help. You'll probably put holes in my roof."

"I'm not going to put holes in your roof." Grateful that he'd worn treaded hikers, he walked up the pitch of the roof.

Noah watched from the sidelines, apparently content to let them work it out between themselves.

"You are going to listen to reason," Caleb told her.

"You're not being reasonable."

"You're a complete novice and roofing is dangerous. How is that not reasonable?"

"This isn't your restaurant, it's mine. I'll be careful, and Noah's doing most of the work."

"You're just as high off the ground as he is. You don't have to be operating a nail gun to fall twenty-five feet."

"I'll stay away from…" Her expression shifted, turning resolute. "Hang on. I don't need to justify this to you. It's my decision."

"Get down off the roof, Jules." There was no way he was leaving her up here.

"Or what?"

"Or I'll carry you off."

"Yeah, right."

"Look at my face. Do you think I'm bluffing?"

"I think you're trespassing."

"You want to go that route?" Once again, he was confronted by her intellect. She was way too smart. Why did she always have to make things so hard for him?

"Yes, I do," she said.

"You can."

"I know I can."

"But what about this?" He was fully aware that brute force wasn't going to succeed. "I help Noah up here, and you help Melissa down there. You get my free labor and the irony that goes with that."

It was obvious his offer gave her pause.

"You'll get more done," he said.

"Stop making sense."

He fought a smirk. "I'm only forced to do that because you're so stubborn."

"I'm not stubborn. I'm independent."

"Noah?" Caleb called over his shoulder. "Would you rather have Jules help you or me help you?"

"You have any idea what you're doing?" Noah asked.

"Yes."

"Then you."

"I've got Noah's vote," Caleb said to Jules.

"Since when is this a democracy?"

"He's right," Melissa called from the patio. "We'll get more done if Caleb helps us."

Jules kept her gaze on Caleb while she answered. "He's up to something. Watfords don't help you. They stab you in the back."

Caleb blew out a breath of frustration. "You honestly think I had time in the past five minutes to come up with a master plot to do you some kind of harm by roofing?"

"You've got the cunning gene."

He pulled out his phone. "Tell you what. I'll sweeten the deal." He pressed Matt's speed dial. "I'll get us another guy and speed things up even more."

"Who are you calling?" she asked, but Caleb was already speaking to Matt.

He quickly sketched out the problem and ended the call. "Matt's heading over," he told Noah.

Jules's face had gone a shade darker with her anger. She was even prettier if that was possible.

"You are an unbelievable bully," she told him.

He leaned in close, lowering his voice. "Now that I've seen that beautiful body, I can't bear the thought of anything happening to it."

She sucked in a breath of obvious shock.

He pulled back and put a hand on her shoulder. "Please get down off the roof, Jules. It's more dangerous than you know. And I truly don't want you to get hurt."

"He's right," Noah said. "Facts are facts. We've got two capable volunteers, it makes sense they should do the work up here."

"Okay," Jules said tightly, clearly reluctant to give in to logic and reason. Then she leaned close to Caleb's ear. "Don't you *dare* bring that up again."

She was right to be annoyed. He truly wanted to keep his promise to leave San Francisco in San Francisco. But he wasn't sure if he could. They'd made love. He couldn't undo it, and he sure couldn't forget it.

She was in his head and under his skin. He liked her, and he desired her. In his weaker moments, he found himself contemplating a relationship with her. But that wasn't about to happen. They were locked in a battle only one of them could win.

She climbed down the ladder and disappeared inside with Melissa.

"I wasn't sure which way that would go," Noah said to Caleb.

"Neither was I."

"She definitely doesn't trust you."

"Yet, she trusts you." Caleb glanced around to see shingle bundles and strips of flashing.

"I'm not trying to destroy her business."

"I've never killed anybody." As soon as the taunt was out, Caleb regretted it.

But Noah seemed to take it in stride. "Put that on your résumé, do you?"

"That was out of line."

Noah gave a shrug. "Nothing I haven't heard before."

Caleb hesitated over his next words. But because it was all wrapped up in Jules, he dived in. "I'll understand if you don't want to tell me what happened."

Noah extracted a blade from his tool belt and headed

for a bundle of shingles. "It was my stepfather. He attacked my sixteen-year-old sister. I stepped in and stopped him, and he grabbed a knife." Noah raised his bare forearm. "I got a scar, and he hit his head on the way down."

"So, totally self-defense." Caleb couldn't understand why Noah had gone to jail at all.

"My sister mentally blocked the attack, so I didn't have a witness."

"Did she ever remember?" Caleb was thinking Noah might be able to get his record expunged.

"I hope she never does."

"Okay, now I trust you, too."

Noah gave a wry smile. "Not my priority, but I'll take it."

"I'm trying to find a way through this, you know." For some reason Caleb wanted to explain himself to Noah.

"Nothing to do with me," Noah said, shifting the bundle of shingles.

"She's better off with Neo down the street than being out here all on her own."

"You mean they're better off?"

"Yes, them. I meant both of them." Caleb hoped Noah wasn't too perceptive. But just in case, he gave himself some cover. "Melissa's been the reasonable one all along. I think part of her is on my side."

Noah scoffed a bit at that.

Caleb found himself curious. "You don't agree?"

Had Melissa said something to Noah? Was she only humoring Caleb by seeming agreeable?

"She knows her own mind," Noah said, cutting the black straps that held the shingles in a bundle.

"Has she said something? About me, my offer, Neo?"

"She admires your success with Neo."

Caleb guessed there was more to that statement. "But?"

"She's excited about the Crab Shack, and she's loyal to her sister."

"But she *can* see there's a path forward with me?"

If Melissa could understand what was in everyone's best interest, there was still a chance she'd help convince Jules.

"I don't know what you think she's told me," Noah said. "We're not exactly best pals. I work, she... Well, she does as much as she can. But she's here every day, and she never complains."

"And, Jules?" Despite himself, Caleb had to ask.

"Jules is a force of nature."

Caleb couldn't help but chuckle at that. He didn't disagree.

"If I was you, I'd give her whatever she wants."

"If I give her what she wants, it'll cost me a million dollars and my dream."

Noah paused at that, a considering expression on his face. "Might be worth it in the end."

Caleb narrowed his gaze, trying to penetrate Noah's poker face. Had he somehow guessed at Caleb's feelings for Jules?

That was impossible, because Caleb didn't have feelings for Jules. Okay, he had *feelings* for her. But a million dollars and his life's dream? After only one night? Not a chance.

While the sun was setting over the ocean, TJ Bauer had arrived at the Crab Shack carrying boxes of pizza and a bag of soft drinks. Jules found it hard not to like Caleb's friends. She didn't know why Matt had dropped everything at the marina today to help out, and TJ acted like it was the most natural thing in the world to spring for dinner for a group of people, half of whom he barely knew.

They were all good-humored about the situation, concerned about Melissa's healing hand and even joking with Noah.

TJ had set the food on the drop cloth–covered bar and invited everyone to dig in. Jules would admit to being starving. She'd scooped a slice of Hawaiian and plunked into a chair near one of the picture windows, setting a cold can of cola on the wide sill.

Caleb approached, using his foot to push a second chair close to her.

"I feel like I need to thank you," she said as she took a first bite.

The three men had finished over half the roof today.

"But you're not feeling grateful?" he asked as he sat down.

"What I'm feeling is confused." She'd been mulling the possible reasons for his help all day, but had come up with nothing. "This seems out of character for you."

"What makes you think you know anything about my character?"

She bought herself some time by taking a bite of the pizza. It was heavenly. She didn't want to insult him. He'd been a huge help today, as had Matt. But she didn't trust him either. Nothing he did would come without strings attached.

She composed an answer in her head. "I know you're willing to put me out of business."

He shook his head. "I'm trying very hard not to do that."

"Pretend all you want, Caleb, but you're threatening to close my road."

"I haven't done it yet. And I don't want to. I've told you that."

"I don't believe you."

"What part don't you believe?"

"That you care anything about me. You want what you want, and you don't care how you get it."

He stretched out his legs, leaning back in his chair. "Think that statement through, Jules."

"Don't patronize me." There was nothing wrong with her thought processes.

He took a bite of his pizza and followed it up with a swallow of his soda.

She hesitated for a minute, but then did the same. She was tired and she was hungry, and arguing with Caleb wasn't going to get her anywhere. She let her gaze wander the room.

Noah was talking with Matt, while Melissa seemed to be engrossed in something TJ was saying. Noah was playing it cool, but his attention kept flicking to Melissa. It was obvious he was attracted to her, but so far he hadn't made any kind of a move. He was polite, but he didn't flirt, and he didn't seek her out.

"Did you tell Melissa?" Caleb asked.

"Tell her what?"

He didn't answer, and she turned to look at him. His expression made it clear where his thoughts had gone.

Jules fought annoyance. Then she fought arousal.

She bit down hard on the pizza. She wasn't going to do this. *They* weren't going to do this. Her tone was tart when she spoke. "Why would I tell her about something that never happened?"

"I thought sisters shared things."

"Irrelevant information? No, we don't share that."

"You can't seriously pretend it never happened."

"Yes, I can."

That had been their deal. It had been crystal clear, and he'd agreed to it.

"Okay," he said, amusement in his voice.

"This is what I mean about your character," she said, feeling the need to fight. "You say one thing, and then you do the opposite."

"I've had a week to think about it."

"You're exactly like your grandfather. A gentleman's agreement, a handshake deal means nothing to you."

He lowered his voice. "You and I are not a couple of gentlemen, and we did a heck of a lot more than shake hands."

"*You're* certainly not a gentleman."

"At least I'm honest."

She huffed out an exclamation of incredulity.

"I can't stop thinking about you, Jules."

"Can we just eat our pizza?" She hadn't stopped thinking about him either. But she had to stop. She had to find a way to get back on an even keel. Too much depended on her keeping her distance from him.

"Are you going to tell me it meant nothing to you?" he asked.

She desperately wished she could. "It meant what it meant. It was a thing at a time and a place, and that's that."

"I have no idea what you just said."

"I just told you to back off. A deal is a deal, and we made one, and I expect you to honor it."

"Circumstances change," he said.

She got to her feet. She couldn't do this anymore.

"Matt," she said in a bright voice, walking toward

him. "Thank you so much for helping today. I can't believe how much work you guys got done."

"My pleasure," he said.

"It can't have been a pleasure. It was eighty-five degrees out there."

"I'm happy to help out. I'll be back tomorrow to finish."

"You don't need to do that. You must have a lot of work at the marina."

Matt's glance went past her shoulder, obviously looking for a signal from Caleb.

"I insist," Matt said smoothly. "We're neighbors, after all."

Feeling suddenly uneasy, Jules glanced to TJ to find he was closely watching the exchange. She turned sideways to catch Caleb in her peripheral vision. There was an undercurrent in the room.

She felt like she was missing something. She probably was. Nobody was this neighborly without an ulterior motive. Stopping by with a Bundt cake, sure, but reroofing a building?

They all looked innocent, maybe too innocent.

"It'll save you a whole lot of money," Noah said.

"You're such a huge help," Melissa put in cheerfully.

If there was an undercurrent, it was clear Melissa wasn't picking up on it.

"We can't impose on you," Jules said.

Melissa moved to take her by the arm. "Why are you being so difficult?"

"I'm not being difficult." The real question was why Melissa was accepting their help so easily.

"They're going to finish our roof."

"They're going to want something in return." Jules moved her gaze to Caleb. "I don't trust any of them."

Melissa frowned in reproach. "Now, that's just rude."

"You're looking for something that isn't there," Caleb said.

"No strings attached," Matt said.

"All I did was bring pizza," TJ said.

"I should pay you for that." Jules moved from Melissa, glancing around the room for her bag. She'd tossed it somewhere this morning.

She felt Caleb's arm slip under hers. "Stop," he whispered in her ear.

She paused. She took in the four other faces in the room. TJ looked affronted. Matt looked amused. Melissa seemed embarrassed, and even Noah looked surprised.

She realized none of them knew about her and Caleb. None of them knew how precarious her hold on independence had become. None of them knew that with every second that passed he entwined himself more tightly into hers and Melissa's lives.

He might have promised not to cozy up to her sister, but he was still being extraordinarily nice to her. He seemed to think that if he did it in front of everyone, he wasn't breaking his promise.

Jules tried to remember their exact words when she'd agreed to the date. But she couldn't. And she couldn't hold him to something she didn't remember for certain.

She centered herself and decided it was best to let things slide. She'd regroup later.

"Fine," she told them all. "Thank you all very much. Your help is making a big difference."

Everybody smiled, and Jules forced herself to smile in return. But something terrible was going to happen. She could feel it in her bones.

* * *

"Are you saying you're ready to pull the pin?" Matt asked Caleb.

It was morning nearly two weeks later, and the two men were on the Whiskey Bay Marina pier where Matt had just finished a pre-charter inspection of one of his largest yachts, *Orca's Run*.

"Bernard has the paperwork ready for me to sign."

"But?" Matt seemed to spot something on the dock in front of him.

He crouched down and pulled his multitool from the case on his belt.

"Would you do it?" Caleb asked.

He'd lain awake last night mapping the likely outcomes of his rescinding the Crab Shack's easement. The lawyers, a protracted court case, Jules's anger, her disappointment, her eventual bankruptcy because she'd spend all her money fighting him.

Why on earth did she have to be so stubborn?

"I'd have done it already." Matt tightened the bolts on a piece of stainless steel mooring hardware.

"You would?" The answer surprised Caleb.

Matt wasn't a hard-nosed man. He was normally more compassionate than Caleb. TJ, now, TJ saw the world in dollar signs alone.

"If all I cared about was my business." Matt rose. "And I *know* how much you care about the Whiskey Bay Neo location."

Caleb gazed over the sparkling waves, wondering if he was being a fool. "I can't bring myself to destroy her."

"You've given her options A, B and C."

"More than once."

"She knows the risks."

"I keep thinking there has to be an option D or an option E. There must be something I haven't thought of that'll break the impasse."

Matt's mechanic Tasha Lowell approached along the dock. "I've signed off on *Orca's Run*," she said to Matt.

"Tip-top shape?" Matt asked her. "It's for a beach-head client from the Berlin show."

"I'm aware of that."

"The guy has contacts all over Europe. He has influence, and can send us dozens of new clients. We need this cruise to go off without a hitch."

She gazed at the sky, as if praying for strength. "I know that. That captain knows that. *Everybody* knows that."

"Is that sass?"

"It's an update," she said.

"It sounded like sass."

"Well, you're stressing everybody out. Chef Morin was just yelling at the steward, something about Alaskan king crab. Poor kid nearly wet his pants."

Matt's gaze went to the office building. "Do I need to—"

"Gads, *no*," Tasha said. "Stay out of the way."

Caleb couldn't help enjoying the exchange. Tasha might be rough around the edges, but she was also smart and fearless. Caleb liked that.

"I am the boss," Matt said.

Caleb couldn't resist. "If you have to point that fact out, something's not working for you."

He caught Tasha's smirk. Her green eyes lit up, and he suddenly realized that under that baseball cap she was quite pretty.

"You're a girl," he began, thinking this might be an opportunity to get some advice.

She immediately seemed to take offense. "Excuse me?"

He wasn't quite sure where he'd gone wrong with the simple statement. "You're female."

She widened her stance in her canvas, multipocketed work pants. "Your point?"

Caleb didn't know what he'd been thinking. Tasha wasn't going to have any insight into how to handle Jules. The fact that he'd even thought of asking her showed how desperate he'd become.

"Caleb is having woman trouble," Matt said.

Caleb shot his friend a glare. "You're not helping."

Tasha pressed her lips together, as if she was holding back a retort.

"It's a business deal," Caleb told Tasha, deciding since he'd come this far, he might as well give it a shot. "I've offered a reasonable compromise, but she's set on mutual annihilation."

"My best guess? It's not a good compromise. It favors you. You're deluding yourself that it doesn't, but she knows that it does."

Caleb took offense to the assessment. "It's the *only* solution."

"Are you looking for my advice, or asking me the secret to changing a stubborn woman's mind?"

Matt laughed, and they both glared at him. He quickly turned the sound into a cough. "She's got you pegged."

"We women aren't stubborn," Tasha said. "We're smart. It just rattles you guys when we're also self-interested. My guess is she's right, but you don't want to admit it."

Apparently having said her piece, Tasha turned her attention back to Matt. "*Orca's Run* is mechanically sound. You should back off now and let everybody do their jobs."

She gave both men a nod.

Caleb watched her walk away. "Well, that was…"

"Emasculating? It happens to me all the time."

"I was thinking illuminating."

"You agreed with her?" Matt sounded surprised.

"I agreed with what she said to you. You do tend to meddle sometimes."

"Ha. I agreed with what she said to you. It's making you nuts that Jules is standing up to you."

Matt was wrong there. Caleb had no problem with someone standing up for their own business interests. What was frustrating him was his hesitation to stand up for his own because he had feelings for Jules.

"I slept with her," he said.

Matt did a double take. *"What?"*

Matt was a brilliant man and a good friend. Caleb knew he wasn't going to be able to give Caleb decent advice unless Caleb was honest.

"In San Francisco," Caleb continued. "She made me promise to forget it happened, and I can't get her out of my mind."

"Wow."

"That's an understatement."

"She slept with you? Was it because of the earthquake?"

"Are you asking if I took advantage of her vulnerability after she was terrified for her life?"

Matt seemed to reconsider. "No. Of course not. You wouldn't do something like that."

"She likes me. I mean, on some level, I know she must like me. She's definitely attracted to me. And she hates that. She fights it tooth and nail. She's really funny. And she's really smart. And sassy. Unlike you, I like sassy. Sassy is sexy."

"I like sassy, too."

That caught Caleb's attention. "Tasha?"

Matt looked surprised. "No. Tasha's...different. And we're not talking about me. Are you falling for Jules?"

Caleb reached out to brace his hand against a pillar. "I don't know what I'm doing. If she was anybody else, I'd revoke the easement, meet her in court, drain her resources until she was willing to make a deal."

"But she's not someone else."

"*That's* my problem. I don't want her to hate me. And I don't want to destroy her. Deep down, I'm hoping for the Crab Shack to succeed. Beyond Jules, there would be a certain justice in that for her grandfather."

"Your family really did pull a number on the Parkers."

"According to Jules, it might be even worse than I thought."

"Yeah?"

"My father." Caleb hesitated to share too much of what Jules had told him. He didn't care about his father's reputation, but it wasn't really his story to tell. "Let's just say Roland Parker might have had a really good reason to throw the first punch."

"Why doesn't that surprise me?"

"Because you've met my father?"

The wind blustered across the dock, and the line of gleaming white yachts bobbed against the bumpers, making hollow clunks on the incoming tide.

"What are you going to do?" Matt asked.

"I truly don't know. I'd considered reasoning with Melissa."

"Melissa seems great."

"She's the more reasonable of the two. But Jules warned me off, and I promised I wouldn't try to co-opt Melissa."

"Why would you promise that?"

"It was the only way to get Jules to come to San Francisco."

There was amusement in Matt's tone. "You bargained away your best play to spend time with Jules?"

"I did." It was as simple as that.

He'd wanted to be alone with Jules, but it sure hadn't worked out the way he'd expected.

It had been better, so much better. It had been amazing. But the aftermath was killing him.

# Eight

It wasn't the first time Jules appreciated the pot lights along the trail from the Crab Shack to the house. It was nearly nine o'clock and full-on dark as she and Melissa made their way home. The sky was black, and the wind was coming up, a storm moving in from the Pacific.

The distinctive sound of Noah's pickup truck faded to nothing behind them as he turned off their access road and headed up to the highway. They'd been refinishing the wood floor today, and the work was heavy. Jules was tired, focusing on putting one foot in front of the other and wishing they had a proper bathtub at home. She'd give a lot for an hour-long soak before she fell into bed.

Her mind went on a tangent to the giant tub at the hotel in San Francisco. But she quickly banished the memory. The last thing she wanted to think about was Caleb.

"Did something happen when you visited Dad?" Melissa asked her.

The question seemed to come out of the blue.

"What do you mean?"

"You've been off. And I realize it's since you got back. You're a little blue and unhappy. Did he get inside your head?"

"Nothing more than usual." Jules didn't want to consider the lingering memories of sleeping with Caleb might be affecting her. "Dad blames me for leading you astray."

"You know that's not true."

Jules linked her arm with Melissa's. "Sometimes I wonder. If it wasn't for me, would you be here?"

Melissa could use her business degree in any number of industries. Jules was the one who'd become a chef. She was the one who'd spent hours as a teenager sitting inside the closed-down Crab Shack, musing on its possibilities. And she was the one who'd promised her grandfather they'd reopen.

"I suppose you are the more passionate of the two of us."

The answer gave Jules pause. "Are you having second thoughts?"

"No. Not second thoughts. But you have to admit, we're in pretty deep financially. And lately you seem so tired."

"I'm not tired. Okay, I'm tired right now. But that's from working on the floor all day long."

The trail became steeper as they approached their house.

"Are you sure that's all it is?" Melissa asked.

"I'm positive." If Jules was coming across as blue, she was simply going to readjust her attitude. She wasn't

truly blue, and there was nothing messing with her enthusiasm for the Crab Shack, not Caleb or anything else.

"Because we have options, you know."

Unease rose in Jules. She slowed to a stop, turning
to face Melissa. "What do you mean we have options?"

Had Caleb somehow gotten to Melissa? If he had,
there was going to be trouble, Jules vowed.

Melissa kept walking as if they were having a perfectly ordinary conversation, and Jules had no choice
but to move with her.

"Noah said something interesting today. I was talking to him. Okay, I was flirting with him. But I think
I'm losing my touch. I'm acting like a schoolgirl, and
it's like he's completely oblivious."

"You really have a thing for him, don't you?" Jules's
heart went out to her sister, and she relaxed a bit, far
more comfortable with the topic of Noah than with any
talk of options for the Crab Shack.

"Who wouldn't? He's so, I don't know, solid, laid-
back. Nothing rattles that guy. You've seen that, right?"

Noah was always there, lifting, carrying, power tools
reverberating through the building. He'd become background noise.

"I can't say that I've paid all that much attention."
Jules was usually focused on what she was doing herself.

"He's so efficient," Melissa continued. "He makes it
look easy, but he gets a ton of work done."

Jules agreed with that. "We're lucky we hired him."

"And his hands. I have a thing for his hands. They're
so capable. You know, scarred, callused, big, über-sexy."

Jules couldn't help but smile at her sister's confession.

"But he won't notice me." Melissa sounded both ear-
nest and sorry for herself. "Why won't he notice me?"

"Maybe you're trying too hard. Guys usually want what they can't have." Jules shrugged. "Maybe don't be so obvious. Let him chase you for a while."

"And if he doesn't?"

"You're no further behind."

"Hmm. I could try that. I have to say, he did come up with a good idea."

"Tell me." Jules felt like a better big sister than she had a few minutes ago.

"Noah thinks we should consider selling to Caleb."

Jules stopped dead on the pathway. "Sell Caleb the Crab Shack? Why would we do that? Why would he even want it? We're not in the market to sell. We're in the market to succeed. What's Noah even talking about?"

"He figures Caleb would easily give us jobs at Neo. You could be a chef. I could go into management. We could make it part of the deal that he had to give us careers."

Jules couldn't believe what she was hearing. "We'd bribe Caleb to employ us? We'd help *the Watfords* make Neo even more successful and give up the Crab Shack?" She tried to imagine her grandfather's reaction. "You know Caleb would bulldoze the place."

Had Melissa lost her mind?

"We need to be realistic." Melissa's voice was small.

"We are being realistic."

"Are we? We didn't count on court costs."

Jules swallowed. "We'll manage."

"Noah says—"

"What's with Noah? He's a carpenter. What does he know about running a restaurant? I know you're attracted to him, but you're the one with the business degree."

The hurt expression on Melissa's face was clear. "This has nothing to do with me being attracted to him."

Jules immediately felt terrible. "I'm sorry. I'm just trying to figure out why Noah would…" And then it hit her. This wasn't Noah's idea.

This idea had Caleb written all over it. It played right into his hand. Caleb had to be using Noah as an unwitting conduit to Melissa, and Melissa as a conduit to Jules.

Jules closed her eyes and gave her head a shake.

"I'm sorry," she told Melissa, re-centering herself and opening her eyes. There was no point in addressing this with anyone but Caleb. Everyone else was perfectly innocent. "It's an interesting suggestion," she continued. "And I shouldn't have gotten upset like that. But I don't think we need to give up. Not yet. The easement case may go more smoothly than we're anticipating. Caleb could even be bluffing."

Melissa looked decidedly hesitant. "You think?"

"It's a possibility. Let's not make any rash decisions." They were in front of their house, but Jules was too restless to go inside. "You know, I'm going to walk awhile longer."

"You're mad at me."

Jules shook her head. "I'm not mad. I'm sorry if I sounded mad. This is your decision as much as it is mine."

"It was only an idea."

"And I only need to clear my head. I'll just walk."

"If you're sure."

"I'm sure. I'll see you in a while."

Jules wasn't angry with Melissa. She wasn't even angry with Noah. There was only one person to blame for this, and he had a lot of explaining to do.

* * *

Caleb didn't often drink brandy. Beer was his bar beverage of choice. Wine was nice with an elegant dinner, and he enjoyed the occasional single malt.

Brandy was soothing. He supposed it wasn't often that he needed to be soothed.

He'd signed the paperwork tonight. Tomorrow Bernard would take the documents to the land office and rescind the easement for the Crab Shack. Then, it would be up to Jules to take him to court. She'd need a lawyer. And it would cost her money she didn't have. And she would probably never forgive him.

Slumped on the sofa in his living room, he stared out at the ocean. Rather, he stared in the direction of the ocean. The clouds were thick tonight, rain splattering on his windows, splashing on the dimly lit deck. Jazz floated from his speakers. The volume was low. Again, it was soothing.

He took another drink of the brandy, hoping it wouldn't turn to acid in his stomach.

Someone banged on his door. The sound was jarring and annoying.

He glanced at his watch, wondering who would stop by. Matt and TJ wouldn't knock, and other people would phone or text first.

The sharp, rapid knock came again.

He set down the snifter and rolled to his feet. He supposed an interruption wasn't the worst thing in the world. Whatever it was might take his mind off his guilt for a moment.

He followed the hall to the foyer and swung open the door.

It was Jules.

She was wet from the rain that was now streaming

down hard, and she looked angry. Her glare was punctuated by a rumble of thunder behind her.

"What's wrong?" he asked.

He knew she couldn't possibly know about the easement. Only he and Bernard were aware that he'd signed the documents.

"I need you to be honest with me."

"Honest about what?" He wouldn't let himself believe it was the easement.

"About using Noah to push your agenda."

Caleb was baffled by the statement. "Come in," he said instead of responding.

She walked stiffly through the doorway, her hair wet, her T-shirt clinging to her body.

"We had a deal," she said. "You promised."

"Jules, you're soaking wet. Come in and dry off."

"Who cares if I'm wet? Being wet is nothing."

He ducked into the guest bathroom and retrieved a towel, holding it out to her.

She didn't take it. "How could you?"

"What do you think I did?" He resisted an urge to dry her hair.

"Don't play dumb, Caleb."

"I'm not playing anything." He looped the towel around her shoulders.

She grasped the ends and backed away from him. "I'm talking about Noah, about how you manipulated him. He's now told Melissa that selling you the Crab Shack is our best move."

Caleb rolled the idea around in his head. It was quite brilliant, but it wasn't his idea. Why hadn't he thought of it? He could buy the place outright, and solve every one of his problems. Jules and Melissa would have the money to start any business they liked.

"I didn't suggest that to Noah," he said.

"Come on, Caleb. I knew you offering free labor to fix the roof was too good to be true. You had two full days up there, you and Matt, to co-opt Noah to your cause."

"I *didn't*. We didn't." Caleb wouldn't have done it covertly. "If I wanted to buy your property, I'd have come out and asked you."

The words seemed to give her pause. "I wish I could believe that."

"You can."

She looked miserable.

"Are you okay?" he asked.

"No." She stiffened. "I'm *not* okay. You're trying to destroy my dream."

He couldn't argue with that. He was trying to destroy her business, and along with it her dream. But Noah had nothing to do with it.

"I've been up-front with you," he said. "All along, I've been honest about my desires and my intentions. Why would I go behind your back now? Why would I use Noah—who I barely know, by the way. Why?"

"Because you thought it would work."

"Rescinding the easement will work."

"It won't get you out of the noncompete."

"But it'll trap you in a corner." He gave in to his impulse, removed the towel from her shoulders and pressed it to her wet hair. "You'll give in. You'll have no choice."

Surprisingly, she didn't seem to notice what he was doing. "I could win in court."

"You're not going to win, Jules. You'll be bankrupt before the first hearing. I have a simple path forward—why would I use Noah?"

She seemed to hesitate again. "Speed?"

"I hadn't thought of that. It might be faster. But I didn't do it. Whatever your sister said, whatever Noah told her, it had nothing to do with me. I worked on your roof to keep you from potentially killing yourself. Period. That's it. That's all I did."

Her shoulders drooped. "So Noah's against me, too?"

Caleb stopped rubbing her hair, and draped the towel around her shoulders again.

"Noah's trying to help you. He sees the impossibility of your situation."

"It's not impossible." She pressed her lips together. "It can't be impossible."

Caleb told himself to take his gaze off her lips.

She raised her blue eyes to look at him. They were glimmering. "And Melissa?" she asked. "How does she feel? She brought me the idea."

Caleb wasn't sure how to answer that. He tried to be gentle. "It sounds like she wants to sell. She may not be as committed as you."

He couldn't help but hope they would take Noah's suggestion and consider selling. Then he wouldn't have to be the bad guy. He wouldn't have to cancel the easement. He could call Bernard and tell him to stand down. His heart lifted at the possibility. He couldn't help it.

"How do I fight?" Jules asked, her voice breaking. "I'm fighting you. I'm fighting my dad. How do I fight Melissa, too?"

Caleb gave in and pulled her into his arms.

To his surprise, she came willingly, burrowing her head against his shoulder.

Jules couldn't believe she was crying. But stubborn tears seeped silently out of the corners of her eyes, soaking into Caleb's shirtfront. She accepted that he wasn't lying. She was under siege by everyone around her. For the first time, she considered that she might be wrong, she might completely fail. Her heart hurt for her grandfather.

She desperately tried to control her emotions, to slow the deluge of tears. Falling apart in front of Caleb was the worst thing she could do. But she couldn't seem to stop, and she couldn't seem to give up the comfort of his embrace.

It was as if he was two different men. When she was close to him, he seemed rock solid and compassionate. All she wanted to do was lean on him. She couldn't even picture the alter ego that was undermining everything she did. Then when she walked away, she couldn't see his kindness. From a distance he was nothing but an enemy.

She needed to walk away now. She needed some distance. But he was hugging her tight, and she needed another minute, just another few minutes while she gathered her strength.

"It's okay," he whispered, kissing her hair.

"It's not." She hated the quaver in her voice. "It's not okay."

"You can take a break from fighting."

"I can't."

"Just for a minute. Relax." His hands rubbed over her back.

She felt her body soften. Her limbs grew suddenly heavy, and the flutter in her stomach turned to a dull ache.

He must have sensed her weakness because he scooped her into his arms.

She didn't have the strength to protest. She kept her

eyes shut and focused on the security of his arms. There would be plenty of time to fight with him later.

He moved to the sofa and sat down, settling her on his lap.

The storm was full-blown now, rain clattering against the big windows, nearly drowning out the soft music in the background.

She sat still, feeling the beat of his heart, letting the thunder and the rhythm of the rain roll over her. He didn't say a word. His chest rose and fell, and the heat of him seeped into her damp clothes.

After a long time, she tipped her head back to look at him. He gazed directly into her eyes. His expression was compassionate, and his gray eyes were opaque.

He brushed his thumb across her cheek.

Then he smoothed back her hair.

He dipped his lips forward, slowly and steadily moving toward hers.

Her heart rate increased, deepening, steadying. She could taste his lips before they even touched hers. They were amazing, fantastic, breathtaking.

Then he kissed her, and the world seemed to convulse around her heart. Her body strained against him. Her arms went around him. And she opened to his kiss as sound roared in her ears.

He eased slightly back. "Is this okay?"

"No. It's not. It can't be." She felt his arm tighten around her. "But don't stop," she whispered.

"We'll work it out."

"We won't. But that's someplace else. It's something else. This is just this."

He kissed her again.

It suddenly felt as if her damp clothes were cloying. She impatiently clawed at the laces of her work boots, until he took over and stripped them off. He broke their kiss to peel off her T-shirt. Then he stripped off his own shirt and drew her close, skin to skin, heat to heat.

Now that she'd made up her mind, she simply let it happen. The last time had been hurried, but this was to be savored. She kissed Caleb deeply, letting her hands and lips wander over his body.

He seemed to sense her mood, and he worked his way slowly from her neck to her navel, bringing gasps from her lips, and ramping up the passion that heated her to her very core. He slowly removed her clothes, and he removed his own, laying her gently back on the sofa, where he made leisurely love to her.

The rain pounded harder, the room heated up, her damp hair all but steamed in reaction to his lovemaking. The leather was smooth against her skin, and his hands were firm then gentle then firm again.

Their bodies joined, and his scent surrounded her. The taste and feel of him filled her senses. His breathing was a rasp in her ear, deeper, louder, faster. Her body kept up with the pace, until she was floating from the earth, hovering in pure bliss for thrust after thrust before imploding in a cascade of pleasure that had her crying his name.

The room slowly righted itself, and she could tell which way was up.

Neither of them spoke. He turned, balanced her gently on top of him, covering her with his shirt. She wasn't cold. But she liked the cocoon. For the first time in days, she felt at peace.

Caleb would have happily held Jules sleeping on top of him forever. But sooner or later, somebody would come looking. Even as the thought crossed his mind, her phone buzzed. The ring was soft, and it didn't disturb her sleep.

He smiled, smoothing her hair and giving her a kiss on the temple. When he eased out from under her, she simply settled into the heat of the soft cushions. His smile widened. She was serenely beautiful, and his shoulders felt lighter.

He retrieved a blanket from the linen closet and tucked it over her, feathering her mussed hair off her face. Then he took a few more sips from his brandy snifter. Brandy had never tasted so good.

He guessed it was probably Melissa trying to call Jules. He took his own phone and scrolled through the history to find the call Jules had made from it in San Francisco. He put Melissa's saved number in his contacts and called her.

"Hello?" Melissa answered.

"Hi, Melissa. It's Caleb."

"Caleb?" Melissa sounded surprised and a little distracted.

"I wanted to let you know that Jules is here."

There was a pause. "Where's here?"

"My place. She came by."

There was another moment of silence on the line before Melissa spoke. "I don't understand. She said she was going to walk. Caleb, what's going on?"

"She was angry."

Distress came into Melissa's tone. "At me?"

The response surprised Caleb. With a last look at Jules, he moved down the hall to the kitchen to continue the conversation. "Me," he said as he walked. "She was mad at me."

"What did you do? Wait, why is she still there? Why didn't she call me herself? Caleb, what did you do?"

He sure wasn't about to give a complete answer to that question. "We argued." He chose his words. "She eventually calmed down. She must have been exhausted because she fell asleep on my sofa."

There was complete silence at that. He wasn't even sure Melissa was breathing.

"Melissa?"

"Are you *sure* she wasn't mad at me?"

"It was definitely me." He took a chair at the table and set down the brandy.

"What did you do to her?"

"She thought I coerced Noah into lobbying you to sell the Crab Shack to me."

"No, that was his…" She paused. "It *was* his idea, wasn't it? You didn't. You wouldn't."

"No. I wouldn't use Noah to get to you. I know I'm on the opposite side of this, Melissa. But I play fair."

"I don't know why," she said softly. "But I believe you."

"Thank you." For some reason, it meant a lot to him that she did.

"Would you consider it?" Her question was hesitant. "Would you buy the Crab Shack if Jules was willing to sell?"

He paused, remembering his promise to Jules about not using Melissa, and wondering how far he could ethically go in this conversation.

Before he could answer, she spoke again.

"Do you think it's a good idea?"

"From my perspective," he said, "it's a fantastic idea. I'd buy the property in a heartbeat. But Jules feels very strongly on the subject."

"I know she does. Sometimes… I sometimes think she's blinded by her love for our grandfather."

"What is it you want?" Caleb found himself asking Melissa.

"Mostly, I want Jules to be happy."

Caleb swirled the brandy in his glass. "You have no reason to believe this, but I want her to be happy, too."

"What should we do?"

Although he would have loved to use the opportunity, Caleb's conscience kicked in. "I'm not the best person for you to talk to about that. It's a definite conflict of interest. But I will tell you I'm not bluffing about rescinding the easement."

"That's what Noah said. He said you were too far into the project, and you couldn't afford to back down."

"Noah seems very logical."

"I've never met anyone like him."

Caleb thought he could peg the tone in her voice. Noah was a lucky guy.

"What do you want for yourself?" Caleb repeated.

"I want to help run a business. I want to put my degree to work. I want to make a meaningful contribution to something successful."

He read between the lines. "But it doesn't necessarily have to be the Crab Shack."

"I'm not as invested as Jules."

"We could—" He stopped himself.

It took Melissa a moment to speak. "You don't want to feel like we're ganging up on her."

He vividly remembered what Jules had said about not being able to fight him, her father and Melissa all at the same time.

"I don't," he said. "Even if it's for her own good."

"Do you think forcing her to give up is for her own good?"

"I think..." He hesitated on how to frame it. "I know she can't win this fight."

"Unless you give up."

"Why would I give up?"

There was a smile in Melissa's voice. "I'm beginning to figure out the answer to that."

Melissa had ended the call then, and Caleb found himself coming to his feet, moving back down the hall just far enough that he could see Jules. She was unbelievably beautiful. He couldn't believe they'd made love a second time. He couldn't believe she was here.

He stood and gazed at her for a long time.

There had to be a path forward for them. More than ever now, he needed a path forward that kept her in his future.

# Nine

It took Jules a moment to realize she was still in Caleb's living room. She was warm and comfortable. She was also still naked.

Last night came flooding back, and she knew she'd made a terrible mistake in confronting him. It might have turned into wonderful lovemaking, but she was now more conflicted than ever.

She sat up in the morning light, spotting her clothes neatly folded on the chair beside her. She couldn't help but be grateful for the small gesture, and she quickly got dressed.

Half of her wanted to slip out the door and go home. But that would be cowardly. She'd done what she'd done, and pretending it hadn't happened wasn't going to change that.

She heard sounds down the hallway and guessed they were coming from the kitchen. Running her fingers through her hair and gathering her courage, she determinedly walked toward the noise.

Caleb was in a bright, spacious kitchen, pouring coffee.

He looked up to stare at her.

Her stomach lurched with nervous energy. "I have absolutely no idea what to say."

"How about 'morning'?"

"Morning," she said, relieved by his relaxed posture and demeanor.

"Coffee?"

"Please."

He retrieved another cup and poured. "Do you take anything in it?"

"Black is fine." Any form of caffeine was fine with her at the moment.

He came around the breakfast bar, a cup in each hand. "Did you sleep okay?"

"Soundly."

He smiled. "I'm glad to hear it."

The polite chitchat was stringing her nerves tighter and tighter. "Caleb...I don't know what happened last night."

"You mean you don't remember it, or you don't know what caused it."

"I remember it fine."

Their gazes locked as he handed her a cup.

"Good," he said.

"No, bad."

"That's sure not how I remember it."

"You know what I mean." She took a drink, hoping to jump-start her brain. She needed to be fully functional right now.

He gestured toward a round wooden table, with four

padded chairs. It was set in a bay window facing south-west. The storm was over, and the sun was coming up, lighting the calm ocean.

"What do you want to do?" he asked as they sat down.

"Nothing."

"Nothing?"

"Go home, go back to—" Her thoughts went to her sister. "Melissa must be worried."

Come to think of it, why hadn't Melissa called? Had Jules's phone battery died?

"I talked to her last night," he said, then immediately put the cup to his lips.

Jules felt her embarrassment and anxiety rise. Her voice came out raspy. "What did you tell her?"

"That you were angry. We'd fought. You were exhausted and fell asleep on my sofa."

"That's it?"

"That's it."

The morning light softened his expression, and he looked more like a friend than a foe. This was the up close Caleb. This was the Caleb she had to avoid if she wanted to stay sane.

"I did tell her you thought I'd put Noah up to it. And I also told her that wasn't true."

Jules found herself nodding. She believed Caleb when he said that. Which meant Noah thought she was going to fail. And Melissa must still have her doubts.

The aspen trees outside fluttered in the breeze, and the waves pushed against the rocks below. The only sound in the kitchen was the faintest hum of the re-frigerator.

"If we're going to keep doing this," he said.

She sat up straight. "We are *not* going to keep doing this."

"We keep saying that, yet…" He spread his hands.

"This time it's true."

"I should have used some protection." He seemed to hesitate. "But you must be using birth control, right?"

She worked her jaw for a moment. She wanted to tell him it was none of his business, but she didn't believe that was true.

"Hormone shots," she said. "Not specifically for birth control," she felt compelled to explain. She didn't want him to get the wrong idea about her sex life—which for the most part didn't exist. At least, until he'd come along. "But that's one of the effects."

He gave a nod. "Good."

"Caleb." She put a warning note into her voice. "We're not going to—"

"I heard you." He spun his empty cup on the polished surface of the table. "I like you, Jules."

She didn't want to hear this. She didn't want the good Caleb to make her do something stupid. Truth was, if she operated on emotion alone, she'd drag him straight back into bed.

He caught her gaze again and held it. "I'm ridiculously attracted to you, and—"

A sound caught their attention. The front door opening and closing.

"Caleb?" It was Matt.

Panic hit Jules straight in the solar plexus, and she lost her breath.

"He knows," Caleb said.

The panic grew. "He *what*?" She rose to her feet.

Caleb looked like he regretted the admission. "He's a close friend."

Her tone was a harsh whisper. "I haven't even told my sister."

"I didn't tell anyone else," Caleb whispered back as Matt's footfalls grew closer.

"*That's* supposed to make me feel better?"

"Morning, Caleb," Matt said as he entered the room. "Oh, morning, Jules."

"I…" she started, but came up blank and ended up blinking.

"This isn't what it looks like," Caleb said.

Matt held up his palms. "None of my business."

She took another stab at it. "We have a…"

"Love-hate relationship," Caleb finished for her.

"Lust-hate relationship." She couldn't see any point in pretending.

"I really don't need to know," Matt said, pouring himself a cup of coffee.

"You're the only one who does," Jules said. "Not Melissa, not *anyone*."

"I'm not going to tell anyone," Matt said, stopping the pour to look affronted.

"Matt's not going to tell anyone," Caleb said.

Jules realized that who Matt did or didn't tell wasn't the problem. The problem was her conflicted feelings for Caleb and how she was going to get them under control. The other, bigger problem was how she was going to get the Crab Shack up and running.

"Do I need a lawyer?" she asked Caleb.

It was clear from his expression that he'd followed her change of topic. "My lawyer is rescinding the easement this morning."

"Seriously?" Matt asked from the other side of the kitchen.

Caleb shot him a look of annoyance.

"I thought it was just a threat," Matt said.

"I never thought it was just a threat," Jules said. The

words felt heavy as she uttered them. "I've known all along he was serious."

"You left me no choice," Caleb said.

"You always had a choice. You could live with seventeen Neo locations and however many tens of millions that pulls in."

"It's not about money."

"If it wasn't, you wouldn't be doing this."

"What about you?" he asked. "You had a choice, too. Neo and the Crab Shack could live amicably side by side."

"That's not a choice. That's a Watford trying to con a Parker. That's history repeating itself. It's the very thing I came here to fix."

"You are so misguided."

"You just hate it when we don't roll over and play dead."

Caleb's eyes darkened. "You couldn't be more wrong."

"I'm wrong a lot." She rose to her feet, reminding herself all over again how stupidly wrong she'd been to come here last night. "But not about this."

She took two steps back, trying desperately to see the distant Caleb, the one she despised, the one out to harm her. She backed into the wall, but she quickly recovered. She concentrated with all her might, but it didn't work.

She couldn't separate him into halves anymore. She couldn't see her enemy. She saw only Caleb.

"Thanks for doing this," Caleb said to Matt a week later as they watched Noah climb the stairs to the marina deck.

It was nearly ten o'clock, and things had been dark at the Crab Shack for over an hour.

"Are you sure he's an ally?" asked Matt.

"I think so. I hope so. I'm running pretty short on moves, so I better be able to make this happen."

"Jules still not talking to you?"

"I can't get anywhere near her." And Caleb had certainly tried.

Since his lawyer had filed the papers, she was refusing to have anything to do with Caleb. He'd tried three different carrots, and none of them had worked. Now the stick had been an even more colossal failure. If he didn't come up with something new, Jules was going to lose all her money, and he was never going to have a chance at exploring their feelings for each other.

"Hey, Noah," he greeted the man, stepping forward to shake his hand. "Thanks for coming."

"You said it was about work?" Noah asked.

Matt gestured to the cluster of deck chairs.

"Melissa told me what you suggested," Caleb opened as the three of them sat down.

It was a clear night, but breezy waves crested higher than usual as the tide rolled out. The yachts creaked against their mooring ropes, while the flag over the dock snapped in the wind.

"What did I suggest?" Noah asked, his expression becoming guarded.

"That they sell to me. It's a good idea. And she listened."

"It had nothing to do with what's best for you," Noah told Caleb.

"I get that." Caleb guessed Noah had Melissa's best interests at heart when he made the suggestion. "But Jules won't go for it."

"No kidding."

"Melissa explained what happened?"

"That Jules thought I was your pawn? She told me.

You do know that's never going to happen. So, if that's what this is about..." Noah started to rise.

"No," Caleb quickly assured him. "It's not."

Noah hesitated for a second, but then settled back down.

"You want a beer?" Matt asked Noah.

"Are you going to ask Melissa out?" Caleb asked Noah.

"No."

Caleb was curious. "Why not?"

"I'm getting the beer." Matt rose and crossed to the wet bar.

"Because she's a university graduate, and I'm an ex-con with a GED."

The answer took Caleb by surprise. "You're also a licensed carpenter."

"Can you imagine her bringing me home to Daddy?"

Matt handed around the beers and sat back down. The wind gusted, and he settled his cap more firmly on his head.

"You're selling yourself short," Matt said.

"This can't be why you asked me here," Noah said.

It wasn't.

Caleb had a different motive. "If I can get Jules on board, would you consider working for Neo?"

He knew Jules and Melissa respected Noah. Caleb liked him, too, and he admired Noah's work. What he wanted was a solution that worked for everyone.

"Or for me," Matt said. "If it turns out the Crab Shack job ends, I've got plenty of work here at the marina for a good finish carpenter."

Noah looked from one man to the other. "Even if I think you're right, that the sisters should sell, they're never going to agree."

"I can't give up," Caleb said. "Melissa admitted she'd like to work at Neo."

"Melissa's not Jules," Noah said.

"I'm not through trying."

"Then I wish you luck." Noah came to his feet.

"Ask Melissa out," Matt said to Noah. "I hate that you're hesitating over your past."

"He's divorced, so probably not the best advisor on women. But I agree with him." Caleb had seen the way Melissa and Noah looked at each other. They deserved a chance.

"Divorced or not—" Noah cracked a half smile "—I'd rather take his advice than yours. I've never seen a guy get himself into such a mess over a woman."

Caleb wished he could disagree. "If I can't change her mind—"

"It's going to cost you a million dollars," Matt finished the sentence.

"That's not what I was going to say."

Noah polished off his beer. "You're not going to change her mind. And, Matt's right, you're the one who's going to cave."

Matt laughed at that.

Before Caleb could work up a counter-argument for the both of them, Noah was gone.

"Noah asked me out." Melissa was beaming as they laid out copper light fixtures and polish on the drop cloth–covered bar. She lowered her voice, glancing surreptitiously at Noah where he was working outside on the deck. "Your plan worked. I've been staying aloof and playing hard to get for nearly a week."

Jules forced out a smile for her sister. She was genuinely happy for her. "Congratulations. Where are you going?"

Jules wouldn't use this moment to feel sorry for herself. She'd been avoiding Caleb all week. She missed him, but that was too bad. She might as well start getting over it.

"Dinner and a club. Saturday night. We're going to drive into Olympia."

"What are you going to wear?"

"Your black dress." Melissa peeled a soft cloth from a stack and opened a can of polish. Her hand was finally back to normal.

"I suppose that's only fair," Jules said.

"I'll try not to ruin it."

"It's not like I have a right to complain if you do."

Melissa didn't laugh, and Jules looked up.

Her sister's eyes were round.

"Dad," Melissa said.

Jules didn't blame Melissa for being concerned. "Dad's reaction is a whole other—"

"Hi, Dad," Melissa said more loudly in a brittle, bright tone.

Jules realized Melissa was looking past her.

A prickle zigzagged its way up her spine.

She turned to see her father, Roland, frowning in the doorway. He was unshaven, which wasn't unusual. His plaid shirt was open at the collar, tucked into a pair of work pants, and he wore his usual scuffed leather boots.

"Is something wrong?" Jules quickly asked. She couldn't imagine why he would have shown up unannounced.

He glanced contemptuously around the restaurant.

"Do you like it?" Melissa asked, her tone still unnaturally bright.

"It's worse than I thought," he said.

Jules fought a rush of indignation. "It's going to be terrific. We've expanded the windows, refinished the bar." She gestured, but the bar was completely covered with the drop cloth. "We've redone the floor, not to mention all the structural fixes, like the electrical."

"And you've spent all your money."

"Not all of it. Not yet."

"We have a budget," Melissa put in, sounding more confident. "It's all laid out. And we've had fantastic help from…" She gazed through the windows, obviously looking for Noah. "Where's Noah?" she asked Jules. "He was just out there."

"Why are you here, Dad?" Jules asked, dropping her polishing cloth and moving away from the bar.

"Your mail was piling up." He lifted a large manila envelope held in his hand.

Jules didn't believe for a second that was his purpose. "You drove up from Portland to deliver our mail?"

"And to talk some sense into you girls." He gazed around the room again. "But I can see that I'm too late. The damage is done."

"Damage?" Jules raised her voice. "Is that what you call our work?"

"I call it folly," he said.

"If that's the only reason you're here—" Jules began, prepared to send him packing.

"Please don't," Melissa broke in. "I hate it when we argue."

Roland took a few paces and tossed the package of mail on the nearest table. "Then listen to reason."

Jules crossed her arms over her chest. As always, when it came to her father's temper, she felt protective of Melissa. "We've been through every bit of this before."

"Is there a problem?" Caleb appeared in the doorway.

Roland turned and it seemed Caleb recognized him instantly. His brow went up, and his nostrils flared.

"You're a Watford," Roland snapped.

"Caleb Watford, Mr. Parker." Caleb seemed to hesitate, but then stepped forward to offer his hand.

Roland didn't shake. "What the *hell* are you doing here?" He shot an accusatory stare at Jules. "What the hell is he doing here?"

"Mr. Parker," Caleb said.

Roland pointed a finger in Caleb's direction. "I'm talking to my daughter, not to *you*."

"He's our neighbor," Melissa said in a conciliatory tone. "He and Matt—Matt owns the marina—have helped us with the—"

Roland's complexion turned ruddy. "You accepted *help from a Watford*?"

"I'm not my father," Caleb said in a deep, level voice.

"Get out!" Roland shouted. "This is Parker land, and you're not welcome here."

"I'd like to apologize to you," Caleb said to Roland. "On behalf of my family."

Roland's hands clenched into fists. "Did you not hear me? Do I need to repeat myself?"

Caleb didn't move. "We're never going to resolve this if we don't talk to each other."

"We're not resolving anything. There's nothing to resolve." Roland took a step toward Caleb. "Get out of this building and away from my family."

"Dad!" Melissa sounded horrified.

Jules felt like she might throw up.

Caleb raised his palms and took a step back. "I can see this is not the time."

"There's never going to be a time," Roland spat.

Caleb turned and walked away.

Jules shook herself out of her stupor. She realized Caleb must have had a good reason for coming. He'd agreed to stay away, and he'd been respecting her wishes.

"Caleb, wait," she called, rushing after him.

Her father reached for her on the way past, but she avoided him, bursting through the open door.

"Caleb," she called again.

He stopped in the parking lot next to the SUV.

"Why did you come?" she asked, halting a few feet back from him.

Heaven help her, she wanted to barrel forward into his arms. The decision to keep her distance had been the right one. But she missed him, never more acutely than while he was standing so close.

"They've set a court date," he told her, his tone remote. "It's Monday. I came to give it one last shot, to see if we could find a compromise." He nodded past her. "When did he show up?"

"Just now. He's here to tell us we're fools, that we should give up this nonsense and come home with him."

Caleb gave a dry chuckle. "Ironic. He and I agree on something."

"I'm sorry." She gestured behind herself. "He can be..."

"Pig-headed?"

"Stubborn. He's always been that way. He loves us, but he can't see past... Well, you know what he can't see past."

Caleb's gaze unexpectedly softened. "Can you see past it, Jules?"

She'd already seen past it. She'd already seen way past it. But she could never admit that to him. "Not while you're stomping on my dreams."

He gave a sharp nod. "That's what I thought." He opened the driver's door. "I'll see you in court."

He drove away, and she felt pummeled from all sides. For the first time in years, she wondered if she could do it. Maybe her father had been right all along. Maybe she was a fool to get anywhere near the Crab Shack, never mind the Watfords.

And maybe Caleb was right. Maybe she should cancel the noncompete and at least get out of the court case without wasting all their money. There was also the possibility that Noah was right. Selling out to Caleb would at least cut their losses. She and Melissa could take the money and find something else to do. Somewhere not here. Somewhere where she wouldn't see Caleb anymore.

And what about her sister?

How could Jules know what was right? How could she choose?

Noah's pickup was parked at the end of the Crab Shack access road, and he sat in the driver's seat. Caleb pulled over, exiting his own vehicle. He walked up to the window.

Noah unrolled it.

"What are you doing?" Caleb asked.

Noah stared straight ahead, jaw tight, lips narrowed. "Feeling like a coward."

The answer shocked Caleb. "Why? What happened?"

"Her dad showed up."

Caleb leaned his elbow on the open window, feeling sympathy for Noah. "He just kicked me out of the Crab Shack."

"I wasn't waiting around for that to happen to me."

"At least you would have had company."

Noah's jaw tightened even further. "I won't put Melissa in that position. She's not going to have to explain me to her father."

"So, you asked her out?" Caleb guessed.

"I did."

"She said yes?"

The question brought a ghost of a smile to Noah's face. "She was pretty excited. I was excited, too."

"So what's the plan now? Are you going to break her heart?"

"Her heart's not involved yet, and I'm going to keep it that way."

"You can't really be afraid of her old man." Caleb would be sorely disappointed if he'd misjudged Noah so badly.

The look Noah gave him told him he hadn't. "I'd take on a hundred guys like him. It's Melissa I'm protecting, not myself."

"Then you're making a mistake."

If Noah stood up to Roland, he just might win. He had a good explanation for his criminal record. And at least he wasn't a Watford. If Caleb had thought fighting Roland would get him anywhere near Jules, he never would have left the restaurant.

Noah sat silent, his hands clenched around the steering wheel.

Caleb stood between the idle heavy equipment costing him a fortune on the Neo site and the half-finished Crab Shack that meant so much to Jules. He wished he was only an ex-con who was self-conscious about his profession.

"You want to fight for her," he said to Noah. "And you want it pretty bad."

"I want to fight for her," Noah agreed.

"She's waiting. It might be ugly at first, but what guy didn't have some kind of battle with a woman's father?"

"Not like this," Noah said.

"Not like this," Caleb agreed. "But it could be a whole lot worse. Look at me."

"You've got it bad for Jules?"

"I've got it bad for Jules." And it was getting worse. Day by day by day, it was getting worse.

"At least you're a rich, successful guy."

"At least your families aren't mortal enemies. I don't know what you've heard…"

"A little," Noah said. "I get the gist."

"Well, Roland Parker just finished meeting me. I have to think you're going to look pretty good in comparison."

Noah shook his head in obvious self-deprecation. "I really am being a coward."

"You're protecting Melissa. You're just doing it wrong. Get back out there."

Noah reached for the ignition key. "I will."

He started the engine and drove away in a cloud of dust.

Caleb watched the loud, battered truck until it came to a stop in the parking lot. The engine went silent, the waves and the wind taking over. Caleb felt a rush of envy. He'd give a lot to be walking back into that room to fight for Jules.

# Ten

Numb, Jules was back inside when Noah's truck slid to a halt outside the restaurant.

"Well, *there* he is," Melissa said, all but rushing for the door.

"Not that Watford again," her father growled.

"It's Noah," Melissa answered over her shoulder.

"Our contractor," Jules clarified, ordering herself to get her emotions under control.

Noah jumped out of the truck and took Melissa into his arms, kissing her soundly.

"Contractor?" her father asked.

"They're also dating." Jules had never seen such a display of affection from Noah.

"Melissa has a boyfriend?"

"He's not exactly—"

Before Jules could finish her sentence, Roland left the building.

Jules's first instinct was to follow. But she was tired. And this was Melissa and Noah's situation. They didn't need her inserting herself into the middle.

She moved to the nearest chair, sitting down to take a minute for herself. When she let her mind go blank, an image of Caleb danced in front of her eyes, looking handsome as ever.

She dismissed the idea, telling herself to change focus. As she did, her father's stuffed manila envelope came into view.

She reached for it and flipped open the flap, grateful for the distraction.

It was mostly junk mail. She couldn't imagine why her father had saved credit card company solicitations and letters from local politicians. There was a letter to Melissa from her college, which she set aside. And there was a notice for Jules from her medical clinic.

She opened it, finding a standard reminder to book an appointment. She needed a routine physical and her hormone shot was due. She scanned over the date then did a double take.

It couldn't be right. There had to be a typo.

She reread it. Then she reread it again. Dread slowly built up, elevating her temperature, making her skin prickle with anxiety. She searched her memory, desperately trying to pinpoint the last shot.

She couldn't remember. There was nothing in her memory that could dispute the date on the clinic's letter. If she couldn't dispute it, then she had to allow for the possibility that it was right. And if it was right, her shot was late. It was late by over a month.

She told herself not to panic, even as her hand went reflexively to her stomach.

No way. It couldn't happen. Even with a late shot,

the mathematical odds were in her favor. They were far and away in her favor.

They had to be.

The alternative was beyond unthinkable.

Her gaze went to the trio outside.

Melissa was smiling. Noah looked relaxed, and her father was nodding at whatever Noah was saying.

Jules didn't have time to puzzle at her father's uncharacteristic calm. She had to find out. She had to know for sure. And it couldn't wait until morning.

She gripped the letter in her fist and rose from the chair, grabbing her purse on the way out the door.

"I'm heading to town. Need anything?" She didn't look at them as she breezed past. She wouldn't have heard if they'd answered.

She wrenched open the door of the minitruck, panic pulsing through her brain cells.

She couldn't be pregnant. It would be a disaster of epic proportions.

As she headed for the Whiskey Bay plaza drugstore, she forced herself to think positively. She wasn't pregnant. She didn't feel pregnant. She felt like a perfectly ordinary twenty-four-year-old woman.

Okay, maybe a panicky twenty-four-year-old woman. But that would be short-lived. She'd take a pregnancy test. She'd reassure herself. She'd breathe a huge sigh of relief. Maybe she'd laugh at herself. Then she'd get back to worrying about the easement.

The easement seemed like a smaller problem now. It was surmountable. With a sympathetic judge, their lawyer thought they had a good chance of winning.

Perhaps this scare would turn out to be a blessing in disguise. It would put her world in perspective. She'd defeat Caleb in court. He'd be forced to leave the easement in place. And the Crab Shack would proceed as planned.

No competition. No baby. No tie to Caleb whatsoever. It was exactly what she wanted, exactly what she needed, even if the thought of never touching him again did leave her hollow.

She was in and out of the drugstore without a fuss. She checked the pregnancy test instructions, confirmed the timetable, then stopped at the public restroom in the lookout park. It was the place Caleb had brought her for that first burger, the night Melissa had been hurt.

She didn't have time to ponder the irony as she walked past the parked cars. Couples and families and groups of teenagers played and picnicked on the grass. Groups walked along the cliff path, chatting and laughing, their hair blowing in the breeze.

To them, it was a perfectly ordinary day.

Jules was shaking slightly as she entered a stall. Sunlight streamed through the high windows. Disinfectant invaded her nose. A woman and her young daughter chatted as they washed their hands. And down the row a toilet flushed.

Jules tore into the test, discarding the box in the waste bin. She reread the instructions then gritted her teeth, her heart pounding and her lungs rapidly inhaling and exhaling the warm, close air as she urinated on the stick.

She checked her watch, closing her eyes and regulating her breathing as she waited for the minutes to tick past. She concentrated on what she'd do after. She'd have to pick something up at a local store, something that was plausibly important enough for her to have rushed out of the restaurant.

Maybe something for dinner. Her father's favorite

was lasagna. She'd go back to the plaza and pick up the fixings for lasagna. That way she'd look like a good daughter rather than an irrational one.

Dangling the test by her side, out of her sight, she opened her eyes and checked her watch. There were just a few seconds to go. She counted down.

Then she took a very deep breath and lifted the test, half turning away and squinting her eyes like she did in a horror movie.

It didn't help. She could see the result. It was positive.

She was pregnant.

Another toilet flushed. Someone's keys clanked as they set them down on the metal shelf and a tap turned on, roaring into the sink. Voices shouted outside, while a seagull screamed.

Jules stared at the two lines in the test window. How could she have been so stupid? Why had she made love with Caleb? She'd never, ever, not even once mixed up her shot dates before now.

How could the universe have played such a cruel trick?

Her phone rang inside her purse.

It would be Melissa, but Jules couldn't answer. There was no way she could talk right now. She knew if she didn't answer, Melissa would worry.

Melissa was going to have to worry.

She'd probably be happy in the end. Because the Crab Shack would fail, her father would definitely be happy in the end. And Caleb, Caleb would be the happiest of them all. He was about to get everything he wanted.

Caleb was certain he couldn't have heard Noah right. "She'll sell?"

"I just finished talking to her," Noah said as he followed Caleb into his living room.

Matt and TJ were already visiting. They were out on the deck with the barbecue warming up. Caleb had sought them out as a distraction. He hadn't wanted to be alone with his thoughts.

"Why?" he asked Noah, blown away by the statement. "What could have changed her mind?"

He was thrilled, of course. But the turn of events was completely unexpected. They had a court date in the morning.

"Reality, I think," Noah said.

Could it be as simple as that? Had the impending court date made her see reason? Finally? Caleb wanted to believe it, but something didn't quite fit.

"What did she say?" he asked. "How did she phrase it?"

"Just that she thought I was right."

"I have you to thank?" Caleb asked.

"Melissa agreed with me. So did her father, and it made me points with him, big-time."

Caleb had to smile at that. He was genuinely pleased for Noah. At least Noah was having success on the romance front.

Caleb was having success on the business front. He should be thrilled. He really ought to be thrilled. He dragged open the glass door.

"Hey, Noah," Matt said as the two men stepped outside.

"Hi," TJ echoed.

"Jules agreed to sell," Caleb told them both.

Matt grinned at the news. "Fantastic. Should I break out the single malt?"

Caleb wasn't ready to celebrate yet. "I can't figure out why she did it."

"Because of her dad?" Noah speculated.

"Her dad?" Matt asked.

"He showed up today," Caleb said, checking the temperature gauge on the barbecue then turning the knob.

"Seriously?" TJ asked.

"Did you see him?" Matt asked.

"For a minute," Caleb said.

"What happened?"

"We had words."

Matt gave a cold laugh. "I can only imagine. He hates you with a passion."

"He hates my father and grandfather," Caleb said. "It's not the same thing." He paused. "It shouldn't be the same thing."

"Close enough," TJ said. "Beer's in the fridge," he said to Noah.

"How much?" Matt asked.

"Who cares?" TJ said.

Caleb was inclined to agree. He'd pay any price she asked. He'd give her anything she asked. He wondered if there was any hope he could use his generosity to make peace with her. He was sure going to try.

He opened the lid to the barbecue and began brushing the grills.

"What are their plans?" Matt asked Noah as Noah returned to the deck.

"Move back to Portland."

Caleb stopped brushing. "What?" He turned to look at Noah. "I offered them jobs."

Noah gave a shrug. "Jules was adamant."

"What about Melissa?" Caleb had been certain Melissa would want an opportunity at Neo.

"She's staying with Jules."

"What about you?" Matt asked Noah.

"About the job offer..." Noah began.

Matt gave a knowing grin and lifted his beer in a toast. "You're going to Portland."

Noah gave a sheepish smile. "There are construction jobs in Portland. And her father doesn't hate me."

"I'll hire them both," Caleb said.

"You can offer," Noah said, taking a seat. "But I wouldn't put money on it happening."

"It's the perfect solution." Caleb looked to his friends, expecting their concurrence. "Their money problems are solved. They can stay in Whiskey Bay. They love Whiskey Bay." Caleb was itching to go talk to Jules.

Noah seemed to consider. "I'm not sure it's about the money. I think the Crab Shack was Jules's dream for an awfully long time."

"But…" Caleb tried to come up with a counter-argument. But unfortunately, he understood.

The Whiskey Bay Neo location had never been about money for him, either. If it had only been about money, he'd have found another location in Olympia. For years, he'd pictured the exact restaurant in that exact location. It was the thing he'd built toward from the very beginning.

He dropped into the fourth chair.

Jules was abandoning her dream. A month ago, he'd have been celebrating. But now that was unacceptable. Sure, it was important to save Neo. But it was equally important to support Jules.

"Caleb?" Matt prompted.

Caleb looked up. "This can't happen."

TJ cocked his head. "Since you just got everything you wanted on the business front, I'm assuming you mean Jules."

"I mean Jules." Caleb saw no point in denying it.

"You mean because you're in love with her?" Noah asked. "Complicates things, doesn't it."

"I'm not… Yes," Caleb said to Noah, giving in to what could be the only truth to the situation. He loved Jules. "It does complicate things."

"What are you going to do?" Matt asked.

Funny, when it came down to it, the question wasn't even hard for Caleb. "I guess I'm going to lose a million dollars."

"Ouch," TJ said.

Matt laughed.

"It's about time," Noah said.

"What do you know about love?" Matt asked Noah.

"Nothing yet," Noah said. "But I'm trying hard to find out."

"I can still get you some new investors," TJ said.

"I don't need them," Caleb replied.

For now, seventeen Neo locations were enough. His immediate plans had a whole lot more to do with his personal life than with his business.

He realized he could lose the Whiskey Bay Neo and still not win Jules. She might not love him back. She might already hate him, and his eleventh-hour gesture might mean nothing to her. But he was still going to do it. If nothing else, she'd have her dream. She'd be here, and she'd be happy, and that would have to be enough for him.

Jules was beyond numb. It had been three days, and her mind still couldn't comprehend the truth. The ocean roared in her ears as she made her way down the stairs from the driveway to her grandfather's house. Or maybe it was panic roaring in her ears.

She'd wanted medical confirmation. And a tiny part

of her had still held out hope the test had been wrong. It wasn't wrong. In fact, her hormone levels were so high the doctor had done an ultrasound.

Jules was pregnant all right. She was very pregnant. She was twins pregnant, and she had no idea how she was going to explain it to her family. She could never tell her father this was Caleb's baby. *Babies*. The knowledge would kill him.

She should have listened to Melissa a long time ago and given up on the Crab Shack. She'd put her sister through so much unnecessary work, so many wasted expenses. Now Jules was going away forever, and Caleb was sure to bulldoze the place.

"You got what you wanted." Melissa's voice carried from the porch up the stairs. "You won. You don't need to rub it in her face."

"I'm *not* rubbing it in her face." The sound of Caleb's voice stopped Jules cold.

"Our lawyer sent you our price," Melissa said. "It's nonnegotiable."

"I'm not here to negotiate, Melissa. I'm here to give you what *you* want."

Jules knew she should leave, but she couldn't make herself move. She stared at Caleb's handsome profile, unable to look away.

"What we *wanted*," Melissa said, her voice going louder, "What Jules' wanted was the Crab Shack."

"I know," he answered. "And I'm here to give *Jules* what she wants. You can have the easement. You can build the Crab Shack. I'll give up on Neo."

Jules let out a gasp.

Caleb turned.

He saw her, and his dark gaze pinned her down.

"Jules?" Melissa peeked around the corner.

"Jules." There was a sigh of relief in Caleb's voice, and he started up the stairs.

Jules struggled to keep her voice even. She had to hold it together. "No."

His brow furrowed, clearly confused.

"No," she repeated, calling on her strength. "We don't want the easement. The decision's been made."

He drew closer. "Change the decision. You won. You win. I'm giving you everything you asked for."

He was clearly baffled, and he was annoyed. And she was in love with him. And she was never going to see him again.

Melissa started up the staircase. "Jules?"

"It's not just about you," Jules told Caleb. "It's about my dad, and Melissa and me."

"But—"

"Go away," she told him as she leaned against the railing, trying to make herself as narrow as possible on the staircase. The last thing she wanted was for him to touch her on the way past. "Just leave me alone. I don't ever want to see you again."

He stopped beside her. "Listen, Jules. I know I've been unreasonable."

"Didn't you hear me?" Her heart was breaking, and she needed this to be over with.

He stared at her in silence.

Melissa's voice was hesitant. "Jules? Are you okay?"

"I'm fine. Completely fine. And I want to be alone."

She moved past Caleb, and she moved past Melissa.

Caleb stayed put, but Melissa followed her down the stairs and into the house.

"Jules?" Melissa closed the door behind them and touched Jules's shoulder.

Jules flinched.

"What on earth?" Melissa asked. "Dad will get over it. This is our chance."

Jules knew she had to come clean.

Tears threatened, and she sniffed.

"Jules?" There was worry in Melissa's voice as she came around to face Jules.

"I'm pregnant," Jules whispered.

Melissa froze.

Jules nodded, oddly relieved to speak the truth. "I'm pregnant with Caleb's baby."

"That makes no sense."

"It happened in San Francisco."

"You made love with Caleb?"

"He can't know," Jules said. "And Dad can never know. I'll come up with a story, say it was a one-night stand with some other guy. He'll be disappointed, of course."

*"What?"* Melissa was obviously astonished.

"But he'll believe me. He'll have no reason not to believe me."

"Forget Dad. What about Caleb?"

"He thought I was on birth control. I was. The hormone shots. But, I got mixed up." She put a hand to her forehead. "I can't believe I got mixed up."

"You're going to lie to Caleb." Melissa's gaze went to Jules's stomach. "You're going to lie to him about his own child?"

Children. It was children. Caleb's children.

Jules's chest swelled with emotion that she couldn't seem to make go away.

"I'm not going to lie to him," she managed. "I'm simply going to stay silent."

"You have to tell him, Jules."

"No." Jules shook her head. She knew she was making the right decision. "I won't. I can't." The only way this worked was if she disappeared from Caleb's life and kept the secret forever.

Melissa took Jules's hand. She walked backward, leading her into the living room. Her voice went softer. "You're not thinking straight, Jules. You're in a panic. How long have you known? When did you find out?"

"Three days. The day Dad got here."

"Sit down."

"You won't change my mind."

"I won't try to change your mind. For now, I'm just trying to calm you down. Being this upset can't be good for the baby. Sit." Melissa sat on the sofa and waited for Jules to follow suit.

The baby. The babies. Melissa was right. Being this upset couldn't be good for them.

Jules's legs were shaking. She sat down.

It took Caleb less than an hour to figure out his next move.

It took him three more to make it to Portland and Roland Parker's front door.

When Roland recognized Caleb, he looked fully capable of murder.

"Hear me out," Caleb called as Roland started to slam the door in his face. "Please, just hear me out. For Jules's sake, for Melissa's and for yours."

"I'm not interested in a thing you have to say." But Roland didn't immediately shut the door.

"I'm sorry," Caleb said, speaking swiftly, knowing he had only one chance at this. "What my father did to you was unforgivable. My grandfather, too, for all I know. But that's behind us. My grandfather's dead, and my father is far away. I'm not them, and I want to make things right."

"There's no way to make things right."

"Will you let me try? Will you give me ten minutes of your time? Ten minutes for me to make up for six decades?"

Roland hesitated.

"If you don't like what I have to say, you can throw me out."

"I can throw you out anytime I want."

"That's true, but I'm asking anyway."

Roland glared a moment longer.

Caleb waited, edgy as the seconds ticked off. But then, to his relief, Roland's expression softened the slightest degree and he stepped back.

Caleb took the silent invitation and entered the town house. It was small, modest, with a slightly close musty scent. The furnishings were aged, and the carpets were dated. He couldn't help thinking that Jules had grown up here. She'd grown up just shy of poverty, while Caleb had grown up with every advantage. A whole new kind of guilt weighed down on him.

Roland didn't ask him to sit down, so Caleb remained standing in the small foyer. He was relieved enough just to be inside.

"I know there's no way to make up for the past," he opened.

Roland grunted his agreement.

"But I have a proposal for you." Caleb found himself nervous.

He'd negotiated dozens of high-cost business deals, managed countless crises, but this situation had him second-guessing every syllable that came out of his mouth.

"It's a partnership," he told Roland. "A business partnership involving the Crab Shack."

Roland's gaze narrowed and his lips pursed.

"I know the restaurant belongs to Jules and Melissa. But I'm looking for your blessing."

"You won't be getting anything from—"

"Please." Caleb held up a hand. "Fifty-fifty. Like it was before. Like it should be again. I'll work hard. I promise you. I'll work hard, and I'll be fair to your daughters. I'll be respectful and honest in everything I do."

"There's no way I will ever trust you," Roland spat out. "There's no amount of money in the world that will put me back into bed with snakes like the Watfords. Is your father behind this?"

Caleb could feel the plan slipping away from him. "My father has no idea that I'm here. He has nothing to do with my business. And he no longer has anything to do with Whiskey Bay. This is me and only me. May I finish my offer?"

Roland compressed his lips even tighter together.

"I'm not proposing cash. I'm proposing a trade. Fifty percent of the Crab Shack for fifty percent of the Whiskey Bay Neo location. Both restaurants can thrive. Jules doesn't believe me. She thinks Neo will take customers from the Crab Shack. I disagree, and I'm willing to back my belief." Caleb stopped talking.

Roland didn't respond.

Caleb was tempted to keep selling. But he'd made his pitch. More wouldn't help. More might simply annoy Roland further. Caleb forced himself to let the silence stretch.

Roland finally broke it. "What's the catch?"

"There's no catch."

"You're a Watford. There's always a catch."

The catch was that Caleb was in love with Jules, and he intended to use their business partnership to romance her for as long as it took. But that was the future. That was his business. And he didn't think Roland was anywhere near ready to hear news like that.

"I brought the building plans for Neo," he said instead. "If you'll let me, I'd like to show them to you. And, if you'll let me, I'd like to write you a check to hire a lawyer, any lawyer you want, to review the deal and make sure it's fair to you and your family."

Roland's expression went from suspicious to perplexed, and he braced a hand against the wall. "Why would you do all that?"

"Because it's right, and it's fair, and it takes a lose-lose situation and turns it into a win-win. And because Jules told me a few things, about the past, about the Watfords." Caleb paused, framing his next words. "As you might imagine, my father wasn't completely honest with me about what happened. And though I have no proof either way, I believe Jules's version, your version." He paused again, giving his briefcase a little lift. "My father destroyed your dream. Let me give your daughter hers."

Roland's gaze locked on the briefcase.

Caleb took a chance, moving to the nearby kitchen table and opening the case.

Roland didn't stop him, so Caleb pulled out the plans, unfolding them over the woven place mats.

"We've already done some work preparing the ground," he said. "It's bedrock under the building, but we'll need to sink piles for the deck."

Roland came up beside him to look.

"It's two stories," Caleb continued. "I don't know if

you've ever seen a Neo location, but the front windows are the signature feature. Well, along with the seafood."

Roland's aged hand reached out to smooth the plans. "This has to be worth ten times the Crab Shack."

"Like I said," Caleb answered, meaning every word. "This is long overdue."

# Eleven

Jules's heart was breaking. Melissa looked just as miserable, while Noah looked grimly determined. He was packing his tools, loading everything into his truck in preparation to shut down the construction job.

Jules couldn't help but wonder what Caleb would do with the place. Would he bulldoze it right away? Unfinished, she guessed it would turn into an eyesore and impact the views from Neo.

Yes, she decided. That was exactly what he'd do. It made sense.

It was also emblematic of the entire history of the Parkers and the Watfords. The Parkers lost. The Watfords won, and their empire grew larger and larger.

She ran her fingertips over the smooth surface of the bar, recalling the hours of sanding and polishing. It had all been a waste of time. Everything they'd done here had been a waste of time. She wanted to be angry, but she knew she had no one to blame but herself.

Melissa should be angry. Melissa deserved to be very angry with Jules.

Jules gazed across the room to where Noah and Melissa were talking softly, standing close together. Her sister looked sad as Noah smoothed his fingers over her cheek. Jules knew their romance had bloomed. This moment aside, she'd never seen Melissa so happy.

She didn't know what was next for them. But she hoped it was something. She'd bet it was something. Noah didn't strike her as the type to go quietly into the night.

Neither was Caleb. But Caleb had what he needed from her. There was no reason for him to fight for anything anymore, not a single reason in the world for him to even seek her out. Their lawyers would take care of the paperwork.

At least the Parkers would get something out of this deal. Her father would be pleased. Her father would be thrilled. She hadn't called him yet. She didn't have it in her to deal with his happiness.

"Jules?" The sound of Caleb's voice sent a trill along her spine.

At first she thought she'd imagined it. But she turned to the door, and there he was, big as life, looking just as he had that first day he'd walked in. He'd been scowling then. He looked joyful now. She supposed he was, since he'd won.

"We're almost finished here," she told him, imagining he was already warming up the bulldozers.

The truth was, they were completely finished. There were no more excuses to linger. Moments from now, she'd walk away from the Crab Shack forever. She'd failed her grandfather. She'd failed everyone. She fought the urge to touch her stomach.

Caleb strode inside. "I'm here to offer you a new deal."

Her heart sank another notch. "Less money?"

He had her over a barrel, and he knew it. It would be just like a Watford to turn the screws.

"No." His tone was unexpectedly gentle as he moved toward her.

"What kind of a deal?" Melissa asked, joining the conversation.

Both she and Noah moved in, as well.

"A partnership," Caleb said, his attention focused squarely on Jules. "Half the Crab Shack for half of the Whiskey Bay Neo."

Jules parsed his words inside her head, certain she was misunderstanding.

"Why would you do that?" Melissa asked.

"Because I think they're both going to succeed. I wasn't snowing you earlier. We should coordinate efforts. I'm putting my money where my mouth is. We thrive together or we sink together."

Melissa found her voice first, and spoke haltingly. "That's ridiculously generous."

"No," Jules said.

Melissa shot her a look of disbelief.

Jules answered her sister with a hard look. They couldn't stay here. She was pregnant, and Caleb was the father. There was no way she could stay in Whiskey Bay and let him find out.

Caleb gaped at Jules in clear astonishment. "What do you mean no? It's everything you wanted. You can finish rebuilding. You can run the place. I'm not going to interfere."

"We can't," Jules said.

*"Jules,"* Melissa pleaded.

"It's perfect," Caleb said with what looked like mounting confusion. "You get your dream. We all make money. Noah doesn't have to follow Melissa to Portland."

Melissa looked up at Noah. "What? What does he mean by that?"

Noah gave her a sheepish smile. "I can't be without you, Melissa. You're amazing."

She gave her head a swift little shake. "You're coming to Portland?"

He put an arm around her. "You don't think I can get work in Portland?"

In return, she leaned into him and smiled. Jules was forced to quell a surge of jealousy. Caleb standing just a few feet away made it all the worse. She wanted to go to him. She wanted to lean into him. She wanted to wake up from what had become a nightmare of errors and secrets.

"So you see," she managed to say without her voice cracking with emotion. "We're all good. We're looking forward to Portland."

"*What* are you talking about?" Caleb demanded.

Her stomach was churning with guilt and nervousness. "I'm saying thanks, but no thanks. Our minds are made up."

"You should at least hear what he has to say," Noah put in.

Jules looked to Melissa for support.

"It's almost too good to be true," Melissa said.

"It *is* too good to be true." Jules couldn't believe she was losing her sister's backing. Melissa knew the stakes. She knew why Jules couldn't accept Caleb's offer.

"It's not too good to be true. It's just flat-out true." Caleb directed his attention to Melissa, too. "We'll draw up a contract. You get half of Neo. I get half of the Crab Shack. It's as simple as that."

"It's not as simple as that." Jules's hand did go to her stomach. There was nothing remotely simple about the situation.

"What is *wrong* with you?" Caleb moved even closer to her.

"With *me*? There's nothing wrong with me."

He reached for her. "Jules, you know—"

"No, I don't know. I don't know why you're doing this." She looked at Melissa, trying hard not to feel abandoned. "And you, you know this won't work."

"Jules, just listen. Let's consider—"

"I can't." Jules was mortified. Tears threatened and she swiped them away. She'd made a mess of her life. Melissa's, too. And now...now, she... "I'm sorry," she mumbled, rushing from the restaurant.

"Jules!" Caleb called as she passed through the doorway.

She started running. She reached the mini pickup truck, wrenched open the door, turned the key and peeled down the driveway. In the rearview mirror, Caleb was standing in the middle of the driveway watching her roll away.

"What was that?" Caleb asked to no one in particular as Melissa and Noah arrived behind him on the driveway. Jules was disappearing in a cloud of dust.

What had gotten into her?

"She's afraid," Melissa said, coming up beside him.

That didn't make sense. Jules wasn't fearful. She was tough and she was brave.

"Of *what*?" he asked, trying to wrap his head around

the strange turn of events. Jules should be thanking him, not running away.

"Of you," Melissa said.

"Jules isn't afraid of me. She's anything but afraid of me."

Melissa sent him a look of disbelief.

"What?" Caleb repeated. "What am I missing? I gave her exactly what she wanted. I made an impossible situation work. It was a solid plan. It was a brilliant plan."

"She's afraid of her feelings for you," Melissa said.

His brain instantly switched gears. Jules had feelings? Scary feelings? For him?

"What feelings?" he asked Melissa.

Melissa gave her head a shake of disbelief. "Well, it's not that she doesn't like you."

He worked his way through the oblique sentence.

Jules liked him. That was good. She was behaving strangely. But at least she liked him. Maybe there was hope.

"What should I do?" he asked Melissa.

She took a beat. "Be honest with her."

The advice made no sense to him. "I have been honest. I am honest. What do you mean be honest?"

"How do you feel about her?" Noah asked.

Caleb hesitated. "Oh, that kind of honest."

Noah gave him a sympathetic smile. "That kind of honest."

"Get her to be honest with you," Melissa said thoughtfully.

Caleb knew they were right.

They were more right than they realized. Jules couldn't read his mind. She still thought they were adversaries. He'd turned the tables too quickly, and she needed a chance to catch up.

"She's headed up to the house," he said out loud. "She's going to pack up and leave."

"That would be my guess," Melissa said.

Caleb realized he was wasting time standing there talking. He started to walk. Then he broke into a run.

His pace increased as he made the end of the driveway. The path angled up, and he ran harder. It would take Jules ten minutes to drive around on the road. He could make it up the pathway in seven if he pushed. And he was pushing. He was pushing very, very hard.

He took the stairs to her deck two at a time. Then he vaulted over the rail at the side of the house, scrambling up the steep grade to the side porch and the staircase that led up to her driveway.

The parking spot was empty. He dragged in huge gulps of air. He'd won the race. At least, he hoped he'd won the race. She'd better be on her way here. If she'd gone somewhere else, he didn't know what he'd do.

Other than track her down, he acknowledged. He'd track her to Portland. He'd track her to the ends of the earth if that was what it took.

He thought he heard the little pickup.

He cocked his head, holding his breath until the sound grew louder and the blue truck appeared.

She parked, set the brake, opened the door and stepped out.

At the top of the stairs, she spotted him. She froze, staring down in disbelief, her hair lifting in the wind, her dark T-shirt snug against her body, those faded blue jeans clinging to her hips. She was so intensely beautiful.

It looked like she was going to turn and leave. If she did, he'd have to run up the stairs to catch her. He hoped he'd make it. He was in pretty good shape, but he was winded from running the trail.

To his relief, she started down.

"This has to be the end of it," she said as she came to the step above him, seeming more in control. She stared at him in defiance.

"This will be the end of it." At the end of this conversation, she'd have no doubt about how he felt.

"Fine." She gave a jerk of a nod as she passed him to open the door.

He followed her inside, part of him wondering what to say, another part of him itching to get it said.

The house had seemed tattered the first time he'd seen it. But now it looked cozy. He associated it with Jules. And he loved everything about Jules.

"You're afraid," he said, following her into the living area.

"I'm not afraid of you," she denied, opening a closet door and retrieving a suitcase.

"You're afraid of us." He was a little bit afraid of them, as well.

He wanted her so badly it scared him. He wanted her as his business partner and his lover. He wanted her today and tomorrow. He wanted to wake up with her every morning and go to sleep with her every night.

She dumped the suitcase on the aging sofa and opened it up. "There is no us." She marched back to the closet and pulled clothes off the hangers.

"There's definitely an us," he said to her back.

She returned and stuffed the clothes into the suitcase. "Well, there won't be after today."

She was wrong about that. She couldn't be more wrong about that.

"Jules?"

She didn't look up. Her voice was full of snark. "What?"

"I'm in love with you."

"Well, that's just—" She looked up sharply. "What did you say?"

"I said, I love you."

She looked completely baffled, more frightened than ever, and ready to bolt.

"No," she said, her face going pale. She shook her head in denial and took a few steps backward. "You don't. You can't."

"I can, and I do."

She reached behind herself and gripped the windowsill. Her voice was little more than a rasp. "You don't know what you're saying."

"I know exactly what I'm saying. What I don't know is why you're fighting it."

"I'm not fighting anything."

"Jules, what we have together… It's exciting. It's energizing. It's amazing. And I want it forever. I want to marry you." He couldn't believe that had popped out. Then he was glad it had.

He wished he had a ring. He'd rather do this properly. But he wasn't taking it back. He wanted to marry her. He desperately wanted to marry her.

Her jaw worked, but nothing happened.

He gave her an encouraging smile. He was through fighting. It was a complicated situation, but it was as clear as day to him that the next step was a wedding.

"I can't," she finally croaked out.

He wasn't accepting that answer. "Why not?"

"I just can't."

He moved closer, keeping his voice gentle. Whatever had her spooked, they were going to work through it. "Do you love me?"

"I... I..."

"Jules, honey, *what* is going on?"

"Nothing."

It was the biggest lie he'd ever heard. "You can tell me anything."

She shrank away. "No, I can't. Not this."

"So, there *is* a this." He'd known it had to be something. "What's the this?"

Her gaze darted around the room, as if she was looking for an escape.

"Jules, get it over with."

"I can't."

"You can."

She finally met his eyes. "I've done something terrible."

He didn't care. Nothing she'd done would change his mind.

"Most people have," he said easily.

"Caleb," she pleaded.

"Do you love me?"

"It doesn't matter."

"It matters a lot."

Her hand went to her forehead. "All this time." She stopped for a moment. "All these years. I've accused your family of lying, cheating and betrayal."

He reached out and took her hands. "Most of it was true."

She stared down at their joined hands.

"Did you steal something?" he asked, impatient. "Kill somebody? Because Noah did that, and it doesn't make him a bad person."

"This isn't funny, Caleb."

"I know. No, I don't know. Maybe it's funny. Maybe it's not. But I don't know because you won't tell me."

He stopped talking. He had to shut up. She couldn't tell him anything if he didn't let her speak because—

"I'm pregnant."

The breath whooshed out of him. "You're *what*?" he choked out.

Did she have a boyfriend? What had he missed?

She kept talking, her voice going faster. "I wasn't going to tell you. I was going to keep it a secret. I know that wasn't fair, and I knew all along it wasn't right. And, I don't know, maybe I would have cracked and told you eventually. I mean you deserve to know. It wouldn't be fair to keep it from you. I'd like to think I would have told you before…you know…you were a father."

Everything inside him went completely still. "Wait a minute? The baby is mine?"

She drew back. "What kind of a question is that?"

"I don't know. The way you were talking… I mean… It was only a few weeks ago."

There was defiance in her tone. "Well, I'm only a few weeks pregnant."

Caleb's brain was racing. Jules was pregnant with his child. She was pregnant. They were having a baby. Joy obliterated everything else in his brain.

"How is this a bad thing?" he asked, his hands tightening on hers. "I love you. You love me. You need to admit it. Now more than ever, you need to admit that."

"I'm so sorry," she said, her eyes starting to shimmer.

He drew her into his arms. "I'm not sorry. I'm thrilled."

"Thrilled?" she asked.

"Over-the-moon thrilled."

"But I was going to keep it from you. I lied by not telling you. I'm a terrible person."

"You didn't not tell me. You just told me now."

"Only because you said you loved me." She looked down at the suitcase. "I was leaving."

He cradled her face in his palms. "Are you still leaving?"

"I guess not."

"Say it," he told her.

Her entire body seemed to relax. "I love you, Caleb."

"It's about time." He leaned in to kiss her.

"It's only been five minutes since you told me."

"That's five minutes too long."

He leaned in to kiss her, but she put her hand to his lips and stopped him.

"What?" There couldn't be anything else. He wasn't going to let there be anything else.

"Uh…"

"Stop doing this to me, Jules."

"It's twins."

His world stopped again. "Say what?"

"Twins. Not one baby. It's two."

His grin grew a mile wide. "Twice the reason for you to marry me. Right away. As soon as we can arrange it."

"Okay," she said.

"We have a deal? No negotiation? No caveat?"

"We have a deal," she said.

He kissed her then. Finally, it was the kiss he'd been waiting for. The complete and utterly honest kiss that told him she'd be in his life forever.

Jules gazed around the Crab Shack three weeks later, loving every single thing she saw.

Noah had added a crew of three to help him finish, and he was getting ready to move to the Neo site and start work there. The decorators had also finished their work, and new dishes, tablecloths and accessories were being delivered every day.

She leaned into Caleb who was standing next to her. "It's perfect," she said.

"You're perfect," he responded, his hand coming to rest on her stomach. "Have you decided?"

"On names?" They didn't even know if they were boys or girls.

Caleb gave a low chuckle. "On a wedding date. I don't want to wait any longer."

"I know." She didn't want to wait any longer either. She wanted to be married to Caleb.

"We need to tell him."

Jules knew that Caleb's offer to partner on the Whiskey Bay Neo location and the Crab Shack had gone a long way toward mollifying her father. But becoming business partners with Caleb was a whole lot different than having him as a son-in-law. Not to mention the idea of Caleb as the father of his grandchildren.

"Could we do it here?" she asked.

"Tell your dad about us?"

"No. I mean the wedding. I know the court house makes sense. But it would be nice to do it here before we open."

His hold on her tightened. "That's a great idea. We can fly to Portland and tell Roland in person."

"Okay," she said with a nod. "I'm ready to tell him."

Caleb gave her a tender kiss, and she turned into his arms.

Roland unexpectedly spoke from the doorway. "I *thought* that's what had to be going on."

Jules sprang guiltily back from Caleb.

Roland kept talking. "No guy makes a deal that bad without a woman involved."

"Dad," Jules said, her heart racing. "We were going to tell you."

"I imagine you'd have to at some point," Roland said strolling inside.

"I'm in love with your daughter," Caleb said.

Jules elbowed him. Could they not take this one step at a time?

"What?" Caleb asked. "It's better that he knows that, instead of thinking that I'm randomly kissing you."

To her surprise, her father smiled. "I guessed that when you came to Portland."

"You're not upset?" she asked.

"Do you love him?" Roland asked.

"I do."

He seemed to take Caleb's measure. "He showed me what he was made of when he came to see me." He spoke directly to Caleb. "You're not like your father."

"I'm not."

"There's some irony in this," Roland said. "I suppose some kind of justice, too. What with the Watfords sharing their wealth with the Parkers. Your grandfather would roll over in his grave."

"I've proposed to her," Caleb said. "She said yes. We're getting married."

"That's even better."

Jules was astonished by the conversation. "You're truly not upset?" she asked her father.

"I want you to be happy," he told her. "I thought Whiskey Bay would make you miserable, like it made me. I thought Caleb would hurt you, probably cheat you. I thought he was cut from the same cloth as his father and grandfather. I'm happy to be proven wrong."

Jules found herself moving to her father.

She gave him a hug.

She couldn't remember the last time she'd hugged him. It felt slightly stiff and awkward, but it still felt good. "I'm pregnant," she told him.

The words seemed to take him completely by surprise.

"You're going to be a grandfather." She couldn't hold back the smile.

Melissa spoke from the doorway. "Hello? You told him?" She looked worried.

"A Parker-Watford baby?" Roland seemed to test the idea inside his head.

Jules tensed, waiting for his reaction.

"Dad?" Melissa asked, concern in her tone.

"That's astonishing news." Then Roland smiled again. "Congratulations. To both of you."

"You don't mind?" Melissa asked, moving into the restaurant, followed by Noah.

"They are getting married," Roland said.

Caleb moved to put an arm around Jules. "We are definitely getting married. We thought we'd do it here," he told the group. "Before the grand opening."

"Grandpa would like that," Melissa said.

"Caleb's grandfather would have hated it," Roland put in, though he laughed as he spoke. "But that's justice. And I think we can declare an end to the feud."

"I would love that," Jules said.

"We'll start a whole new era," Melissa said.

"We'll start a whole new family," Caleb whispered in Jules's ear.

\* \* \* \* \*

# COMING NEXT MONTH FROM

**HARLEQUIN®**

*Desire*

Available August 8, 2017

### #2533 THE CEO'S NANNY AFFAIR
*Billionaires and Babies* • by Joss Wood
When billionaire Linc Ballantyne's ex abandons not one, but *two* children, he strikes up a wary deal with her too-sexy sister. She'll be the nanny and they'll keep their hands to themselves. But their temporary truce soon becomes a temporary tryst!

### #2534 TEMPTED BY THE WRONG TWIN
*Texas Cattleman's Club: Blackmail* • by Rachel Bailey
Harper Lake is pregnant, but the father isn't who she thinks—it's her boss's identical twin brother! Wealthy former Navy SEAL Nick Tate pretended to be his brother as a favor, and now he's proposing a marriage of convenience that just might lead to real romance...

### #2535 THE TEXAN'S BABY PROPOSAL
*Callahan's Clan* • by Sara Orwig
Millionaire Texan Marc Medina must marry immediately to inherit his grandfather's ranch. When his newly single secretary tells him she's pregnant, he knows a brilliant deal when he sees one. He'll make her his wife...and have her in his bed!

### #2536 LITTLE SECRETS: CLAIMING HIS PREGNANT BRIDE by Sarah M. Anderson
Restless—that's businessman and biker Seth Bolton. But when he rescues pregnant runaway bride Kate Burroughs, he wants much more than he should with the lush mom-to-be... But she won't settle for anything less than taming his heart!

### #2537 FROM TEMPTATION TO TWINS
*Whiskey Bay Brides* • by Barbara Dunlop
When Juliet Parker goes home to reopen her grandfather's restaurant, she clashes with her childhood crush, tycoon Caleb Watford, who's building a rival restaurant. Then the stakes skyrocket after their one night leaves her expecting two little surprises!

### #2538 THE TYCOON'S FIANCÉE DEAL
*The Wild Caruthers Bachelors* • by Katherine Garbera
Derek Caruthers promised his best friend that their fake engagement would end after he'd secured his promotion...but what's a man of honor to do when their red-hot kisses prove she's the only one for him?

---

YOU CAN FIND MORE INFORMATION ON UPCOMING HARLEQUIN® TITLES, FREE EXCERPTS AND MORE AT WWW.HARLEQUIN.COM.

HDCNM0717

# Get 2 Free Books,
## Plus 2 Free Gifts—
### just for trying the Reader Service!

HARLEQUIN *Desire*

---

**YES!** Please send me 2 FREE Harlequin® Desire novels and my 2 FREE gifts (gifts are worth about $10 retail). After receiving them, if I don't wish to receive any more books, I can return the shipping statement marked "cancel." If I don't cancel, I will receive 6 brand-new novels every month and be billed just $4.55 per book in the U.S. or $5.24 per book in Canada. That's a savings of at least 13% off the cover price! It's quite a bargain! Shipping and handling is just 50¢ per book in the U.S. and 75¢ per book in Canada.* I understand that accepting the 2 free books and gifts places me under no obligation to buy anything. I can always return a shipment and cancel at any time. The free books and gifts are mine to keep no matter what I decide.

225/326 HDN GMRV

| | | |
|---|---|---|
| Name | (PLEASE PRINT) | |
| Address | | Apt. # |
| City | State/Prov. | Zip/Postal Code |

Signature (if under 18, a parent or guardian must sign)

### Mail to the **Reader Service:**
**IN U.S.A.:** P.O. Box 1341, Buffalo, NY 14240-8531
**IN CANADA:** P.O. Box 603, Fort Erie, Ontario L2A 5X3

**Want to try two free books from another line?**
**Call 1-800-873-8635 or visit www.ReaderService.com.**

*Terms and prices subject to change without notice. Prices do not include applicable taxes. Sales tax applicable in N.Y. Canadian residents will be charged applicable taxes. Offer not valid in Quebec. This offer is limited to one order per household. Books received may not be as shown. Not valid for current subscribers to Harlequin Desire books. All orders subject to approval. Credit or debit balances in a customer's account(s) may be offset by any other outstanding balance owed by or to the customer. Please allow 4 to 6 weeks for delivery. Offer available while quantities last.

**Your Privacy**—The Reader Service is committed to protecting your privacy. Our Privacy Policy is available online at www.ReaderService.com or upon request from the Reader Service.

We make a portion of our mailing list available to reputable third parties that offer products we believe may interest you. If you prefer that we not exchange your name with third parties, or if you wish to clarify or modify your communication preferences, please visit us at www.ReaderService.com/consumerschoice or write to us at Reader Service Preference Service, P.O. Box 9062, Buffalo, NY 14240-9062. Include your complete name and address.

HDI7R2

Violet, looking messier than Hogan had ever seen her, was leaning over the papers again scattered across her desk.

"Violet?"

Slowly she turned her face toward him.

Her bloodshot eyes surprised him. Sick. He stepped in farther. "Hey, you okay?"

She looked from him to the paperwork. "I don't know." More coughs racked her.

Hogan strode forward and put a hand to her forehead. "Shit. You're burning up."

"What time is it?"

"A few minutes after midnight."

"Oh." She pushed back from the desk but didn't make it far. "The restaurant," she gasped in between strained breaths.

"I took care of it." Holding her elbow, he helped to support her as she stood. His most pressing thought was getting her home and in bed. No, not the way he'd like, but definitely the way she needed. "Where are your car keys?"

Unsteady on her feet, she frowned. "What do you mean, you took care of it?"

"You have good employees—you know that. They're aware of the routine. Colt pitched in, too. Everything is done."

"But..."

"I double-checked. I'm not incompetent, so trust me."

Her frown darkened.

"You can thank me, Violet."

She tried to look stern, coughed again and gave up. "Thank you." Still she kept one hand on the desk. "I'm just so blasted tired."

"I know." He eased her into his side, his arm around her. "Come on. Let me drive you home." Then he found her purse and without a qualm, dug through it for her keys.

He found them. He also found two condoms. His gaze flashed to hers, but her eyes were closed and she looked asleep on her feet, her body utterly boneless as she drew in shallow, strained breaths.

"Come on." With an arm around her, her purse and keys held in his free hand, he led her out the back way to the employee lot, securing the door behind her. Her yellow Mustang shone bright beneath security lights.

His bike would be okay. Or at least, it better be.

Violet tried to get herself together but it wasn't easy. She honestly felt like she could close her eyes and nod right off. "The trash—"

"Was taken out." He opened the passenger door and helped her in.

"If you left on even one fan—"

"It would set off the security sensors. I know. They're all off." He fastened her seat belt around her and closed her door.

As soon as he slid behind the wheel, she said, "But the end-of-day reports—"

"Are done." He started her car. "Try not to worry, okay?"

Easier said than done.

Because the town was so small, Hogan seemed to know where she lived even though she'd never had him over. She hadn't dared.

Hogan in her home? Nope. Not a good idea.

Even feeling miserable, her head pounding and her chest aching, she was acutely aware of him beside her in the enclosed car, and the way he kept glancing at her. He tempted her, always had, from the first day she'd met him.

He was also a major runaround. Supposedly a reformed runaround, but she didn't trust in that. Things had happened with his late wife, things that had made him bitter and unpredictable.

Yet no less appealing.

She wasn't one to pry; otherwise she might have gotten all the details from Honor, his sister-in-law, already. She figured if he ever wanted to, Hogan himself would tell her. Not that there was any reason, since she would not get involved with him.

Hogan was fun to tease, like watching the flames in a bonfire. You watched, you enjoyed, but you did not jump in the fire. She needed Hogan Guthrie, but she wasn't a stupid woman, so she tried to never court trouble.

*Don't miss* WORTH THE WAIT
*by* New York Times *bestselling author Lori Foster!*

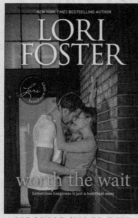